MW01167231

In Her

MakeUp

PHOENIX ASH

Copyright © 2018 Phoenix Ash

ISBN-13:9781723356797

ISBN-10:1723356794

DEDICATION

For all the secrets that birth others. For revelations and second chances. For voice searching. For acceptance. For healing.

ACKNOWLEDGMENTS

God has given me more than has been taken away. I am grateful. Bryant and Saadiya, you fill me with love, laughter, and the best kisses. Nani, thank you for exposing me to the experiences that sharpen my tools and for the dedication that makes my endeavors possible. Jonay Jackson, you make me believe in a better tomorrow. GiGi and Pop-Pop, thank you for being there for our household. Saddi's Grandpa (Jon), thank you for your gentleness and genuine laughter. Nai'lah Carter, you're always there when I need you. Rosa and Tasha, thank you for pouring into me from the moment we met. Shannon Sylvain, thank you for sharing your space with me. Color Comm, you inspired me, you stretched me, you surrounded me with power. Thank you. And Reader, thank you for everything.

1 GRIEF

Cherish wiped her sweat sprinkled forehead across her bare arm. Drying the last of the silverware, she sighed. The snow hadn't stopped falling since they left the burial grounds. Despite the outside chill, the constant commotion of the day's events required her to change out of her velvet, black long-sleeve and into a silk tank top as soon as she made it in the door of her mother's house. She peered at the accumulation between the houses, recalling Brandon's excitement over each year's first snowfall. "Well, Brandon, you must've prayed for it cause it doesn't look like this will let up anytime soon."

"Who are you talking to, dear?" Mrs. Ollie bustled into the kitchen. She lowered another set of dishes into the sink. "Are you handwashing everything? Oh goodness, dear, please have a seat. Let me take care. These can call go into the dishwasher."

Cherish backed away. As a child she learned that debating with her elders, particularly members of her mother's church, would lead to migraines, scripture quotes, and yielding to their will. "Yes, Mrs. Ollie. I'll just go see if them men need more beer."

Mrs. Ollie nodded her approval as Cherish hurried out of the kitchen. At the threshold of the family room, Cherish stood watch. The eight men overcrowded the room, but seemed comfortable nonetheless. While a few sat watching the sports channel the others stood in discussion about the weather and current politics. The buzz of conversation was warming. Brandon loved a get-together with good spirits and energetic exchanges. She imagined him looking down from heaven interjecting his unheard opinions, commenting on the player interviews, laughing at jokes she wouldn't understand.

"In breaking news, a surprise to us all here and I'm sure to those of you at home, Jackson

Trent says he's retiring. In a press conference earlier today, he announced he won't be returning for next year's football season. An unexpected turn of events given his team's near win of this past season's Super Bowl…"

The name Jackson Trent ringing throughout Cherish's ears, she stood erect. A cold rushed over her, the chill like ice picks stabbing at her wrists. Her knees threatening to fold, she managed to lean against the door post. Family friend, Mr. Baylock increased the volume.

"Retiring? You hear this, man? Brandon went to college with that guy, you know? Roommates, I believe. Ain't that right Cherish?" Mr. Baylock hadn't expected Cherish to respond. He kept his eyes glued to the television. He hadn't noticed the color draining from her face or the pee dripping from the hem of her sweat pants.

"Wow! A daughter he says? Pretty noble to go on search for a child you've only just found that you had. Giving up his whole career. Well God bless him!"

The crash of beer bottle glass against the laminate turned everyone's attention to Cherish. Her fingers had gone numb and so it seemed the rest of her did as well. Still with her mouth agape she stared at the player as he thanked the press for attending.

"Let me get this thing cleaned up. Someone get Maddy and sit Cherish down. Poor thing. Brandon could've had a career as impressive as Jackson's."

Mrs. Ollie rushed in, wrapping her arms around Cherish's shoulder. "Baylock, that's enough of that. Hard enough grieving her husband then reminiscing over what could've been. Come now, Cherish. Where's Maddie? The girl won't budge."

At the second call of her name, Madeline hurried to her daughter's side. "What happened, Ollie?"

"I don't know. Maybe it was Baylock and all his harping on what might've been of Brandon's career. The man was as sweet and stand-up as they come. Don't matter what he could've did. He loved Cherish and took care of their family. We ought to be celebrating the man he was cause he was quite a beautiful spirit." She continued to struggle with moving Cherish. "Maddie, she won't move. I'm trying to get over to the sofa. Is Tierra still asleep? Somebody check. Hate for her to catch glimpse of her mother like this."

Just then Cherish broke free of the woman's grip. She raced out of the room, through the kitchen then up the stairs. Midway, she paused, clutching her pearls, attempting to catch her breath. Tears cascaded down her cheeks. *This can't be happening.* She closed her eyes and took seat on the stair. Burying her face in her hands she let the water fall from her eyes, confessing, *Brandon I need you here. I can't do this without you. I just can't.*

2 VISITING LOVE

Seventeen-year-old, Cherish slid her feet back and forth across the *Welcome* mat outside of Brandon's apartment. Her grip tightened around the straps of her duffel bag. *Okay, Cherish. This is the fourth time. You think they're clean by now? Oh my God, are my lips moving?* She looked around. No one was watching. *Oh, I'm just being silly. Everyone talks to themselves, don't they? You'd think I never spent the night with the man before. Well technically I haven't spent an actual night, but come on, we know what the invite was about. It's sex. He probably misses me, but really, he misses my sex. I mean damn, it is magical. So, what am I so nervous for? He's obviously not caught up with any of these college girls or he wouldn't have called me.*

It was Brandon's first semester away at school. They hadn't seen each other in over two months. *It's been seventy-two days to be exact.* The three-minute phone calls after his football practices left them both yearning for the grips of familiar fingertips. They reminisced about nights she'd tutor him in History then follow him down to the High School's darkened football field. She'd run the field yelling questions. He could only get to tag her if he was right on the answer. Quick taps would turn into firm holds. Tugs then turned to embraces. Before the night would end they'd be wrapped in each other's nakedness whispering promises of eternity.

Now Brandon was spending long nights studying in the library, far away from Cherish. His tutor (they agreed he should get a male) told him he was picking up the information well, but Brandon still felt compelled to pace the floor, Cherish on the other end of the phone, each night before receiving his expected graded assignments. "I'm not going to blow this," he'd assured her. "When we get married, you'll have a husband with an education. You will be proud of me. I just need you here, even if for a little while."

Cherish shook her head as she pulled the spare key from beneath the mat. *I'm always proud of you, Mr. Proper.* She pushed the door open. Everything was quiet. A fragrance, an overkill of freshly washed linen and lemon, fanned her nose hairs. She proceeded inside and set her bag down by the door. Detecting the faint odor of musty gym socks Cherish chuckled. She now appreciated the excessive attempt at freshness. *I wonder if they tried actually washing the dirty socks I'm sure they have stashed around here somewhere.* The apartment was dark save for a dim flicker of light from a candle upheld by a dollar store candle-holder, which sat at the center of a card table. Her cheeks flushed and nerves settled. *Oh Brandon, you're a stumbling romantic.* She walked over to find a torn piece of a brown paper bag with a note scribbled on it.

Cherish,

I ran to the store.

Make yourself comfortable in my room

(to the left)

Love,

Brandon

Duffel bag in tow, Cherish proceeded down the rose petal sprinkled hallway. Red, white, and pink, in his typical Valentine's Day color scheme. Cherish grinned as she took notice of the apartment's other details. *That sofa looks to have been rescued from someone's trash. I can't imagine his roommate wanted that. If I know Brandon he sold him on it as a good deed.*

Cracking the bedroom door on the left, Cherish gasped. Her heart thumped with anticipation. Red heart shaped balloons bounced about with the words, *I love you,* printed on each one. *Oh my… One, two, three, four; there's got to be at least a dozen balloons here.*

Brandon was making the weekend feel like a scene from a movie. He was keeping his promise. Cherish recalled the moment she confessed Brandon wouldn't be her first. It took her three weeks to work up the nerve. Not wanting to wait until their first intimate encounter, she met him on the bleachers after practice. Stuttering with a palpitating heart, she revealed what half a dozen boys from her church already knew.

Brandon shrugged. "Nothing to do with me. That's your past. We've all got one." He beamed, "I'm trying to monopolize your future."

Cherish giggled. "Monopolize? Using vocabulary words, are we?"

He kissed her lips. "Whatever it takes to keep that smile on your face."

Making herself comfortable, Cherish sat on Brandon's full-sized bed. *And he even made his bed. Wow! You can bounce a quarter off this. I wonder if the coach makes them all do it cause I know Brandon would leave this whole place in shambles if you let him.* There was a small television propped up on a refurbished armoire. She spotted the remote and turned the television on. After flipping through the channels a few times, she decided to turn it off. It was a pointless effort to contain her anxiousness over the possibility of releasing the heat she'd been desperately trying to keep tamed since Brandon left for college. Although they looked forward to Thanksgiving and Christmas vacations, they found that his commitment to the team wouldn't allow for more than a day home at a time. Admittedly, she did allow her head to be turned a time or two, rationalizing how easy it would be to keep any indiscretion a secret. However, Brandon was her prize and she knew she'd never forgive herself for losing him.

"Okay Brandon, I'm leaving. The apartment is all yours." A voice with the bass of old jazz came from the adjoining room.

Startled, Cherish lunged forward, securing the bedroom door. *That must be his roommate, Jackson. Should I say something to let him know I'm in here? Maybe I should just keep quiet. Too late for that, he probably heard the door shut. Where the hell is Brandon?*

She smoothed her skirt over as she heard footsteps pause in front of Brandon's door. After a moment, the footsteps picked up again but then sounded further in the distance. Cherish was relieved. *Good. That would have been a little awkward to meet like this.*

All seemed quiet again. Without any posters on the wall to study, Cherish found herself pacing the room pausing at every pass of the window to see if she could spot Brandon on his way. *I hate when he does stuff like this. He knew I was coming. What could be at the store that would take him so long? Oh he has a stereo at least.* She fiddled with the knobs, settling on a station playing her favorite song. *There's something in my heart, something in my heart. It's got me hooked on you...*

Jackson appeared in the doorway. "I was on my way home for the weekend when I heard the changing of the radio stations."

Cherish halted her swaying. At six-foot five with the blue black skin and eyes brown like the smoky quartz she studied during Wednesday's Geology Lab, she could now comprehend the tales Brandon shared in which women, both home and away, would literally chase after Jackson with even some concluding with cat fighting at his doorstep. Slightly raised to one side, his smile could suffocate and blind while merely asking for permission to shine. The woven twists of his locks were meticulously scooped in a banded bun as if to hide his tendency towards rebellion against social norms. As if above his shoulders were not enough to inebriate the purest of spirits, his chest bulged firmly beneath the thermal failing at encasing his smolder.

He extended his hand. "I'm Jackson and I hope you're Cherish or I'd be making a fool out of both me and Brandon." He chuckled.

Nervously, Cherish shook his hand and nodded. Her smile was meek as she quietly warned her eyes not to flirt. He held her hand longer than she should've allowed, but letting go wasn't appealing. She tried to look away from his stare but he had caught a glance of her soul. Guilt was on its way. Still, her heart struggled to keep it at bay just for a moment more.

There was a tapping at the front door. The noise stirred them back into reality. As if in silent agreement, each took one last glare to bank in the pits of their memories. A perceived "thank you for the experience" before the drop of hands ended in reluctant parting. Jackson scurried to answer Brandon, whom was apologizing for misplacing his key. Cherish was left to dry her palms and await Brandon's embrace.

3 AWAY FROM HOME

So, this is college. For all of this I could've stayed home and listened to my grandmother's lectures. Tierra doodled her name on the back page of her notebook. Mr. Leonard's monotone explanation of qualitative versus quantitative variables lulled most of the class into a drowsy stupor. It was early October and the allure of Mr. Leonard's boyish green eyes and Spaniard accent had worn off, leaving coma-inducing math teacher in its wake. If it weren't for Tierra's seat by the sun-beamed window and the occasional gusts of wind, she was sure she would've drifted into the kind of sleep that produced snores and incoherent mumblings about fantastical objects.

Tierra peered over at her roommate, Michelle, who had no issue with making herself comfortable. Pink streaked hair and arms sprawled across her desk, her cheek was pressed against the wood. Tierra chuckled. She had to hand it to her. There would be no way Tierra could be entranced in that kind of sleep and not sound like a bellowing rhinoceros or a grunting pig.

I wish sleep came to me that easily. Tierra returned her attention to the swaying trees outside the window. It had been six years since her father's passing. Each day she'd wonder what he'd say about how she'd grown or what parts of her day he'd find humorous. At night she'd sit up in her bed, back against the wall, furious with herself for wondering what could never be answered.

"Okay it looks like our time is up. Please study chapters one through six and be prepared for a quiz on Tuesday." Bags were tossed over shoulders, as students raced from the classroom like taking their time would negate their opportunity to escape.

Michelle was abruptly awakened. "Quiz? T, did he say quiz?"

Tierra smirked, shaking her head at Michelle's panic. *If I love her for nothing else its for the entertainment.* It was nice having someone in her life who wasn't grieving or forcing her to bury her head in scriptures. Albeit a friend who rarely showed up for class and when she did professors were forced to compete for attention with her as a scantily dressed comatose spectacle. Michelle was the only friend Tierra was able to make in the months she had been on campus. Yet, it seemed she was the friend Tierra needed.

Wiping the drool from the corners of her mouth, Michelle teased. "I ask you because I know you caught what he said, Tierra. Was he staring into your eyes while he said quiz, with his lip quivering?" She looped her arm in with Tierra's as the two headed out of the one-story brick building and onto the chilled grass toward their dorm. "You know, he'd probably give you an A if you just winked at him every now and again."

Tierra blushed. Since Mr. Leonard had asked her name after she was the only student to raise her hand with the memorized dictionary definition of Statistics on the first day of class, Michelle had been trying to convince her of Mr. Leonard's crush. Despite Tierra's constant protest of the notion, the thought did help with summoning the energy to attend his much too long, three o'clock lecture. Imagining his dark-haired goatee and wide toothed smile inching closer to her puckered lips in a darkened unattended classroom secretly moistened her underwear. His cologne, a melody of sawed wood and and cooling musk hung in the air whenever he walked past her desk. The scent would linger around her imagination, causing her to dip out and into the restroom. "Shame the only action I could catch is that of a fictitious crush from what has to be the most stale and uninteresting Spaniard Prince to ever touch land."

"You really think he's a Prince?" There was a pause before both girls exploded in laughter. Michelle unhooked her arm and led the way into their dorm room. The two girls settled in to their perspective corners. "Seriously, though, you're all up in your books all the time. How you gonna get anyone's attention that way? You should come with me tonight. Have a little fun, meet a few people."

Tierra lay facing the ceiling. "Who do you suspect I'd meet at a strip club; other than my daddy's ghost looking like an angry belt, chasing my behind up out of there? I'm just going to lay here and enjoy my drama-free life until a fine pre-med Hercules, or maybe even a fledgling archeologist, realizes how beautiful my brain is and falls madly in love with me."

"Oh sweetie, your naïveté is so cute, but please don't get your hopes up like that. It'll break your heart when your Mr. Dream-Come-True loves you in the day then traipses out to see me dance at night." Michelle poked her butt out then bunny-hopped over to Tierra. She grinded her behind up and down the edge of Tierra's bed. Although Tierra fought to hold her breath, she couldn't help but giggle.

"You see you're having fun already. Don't think I'm going to keep giving you these private shows, though." She looked through her wallet then counted out five twenties. "Anyway, come with me to the liquor store. Your old ass attitude is easier for the cashier to believe than my sunny disposition."

"You really think I act old?" Although the question was posed out loud, she contemplated the answer she would've given herself. She recalled her grandmother's graduation day advice. *Listen baby, neither of your parents were able to fulfill this dream but don't you let that knowledge weigh you down. They both made decisions that forced them to grow up way too fast. Enjoy your time away. Make friends, laugh with your gut, and please don't worry about your mother and me. She's lost half her mind with your father gone, but you don't go losing yours trying to find hers.*

4 DEATH AND THE LEFTOVERS

"Cherish, honey where you running off to?"

Madeline's waddle met Cherish at the top of the carpeted stairs. Teardrop stains sprinkling the path, Madeline was careful not to let hers fall as well. Her daughter had always been the strongest person in the room, able to mask her emotions until alone with her journal where she felt it was safe to let them pour. For that reason, Madeline had never pried. Whatever it was that Cherish was jotting, it was helping her cleanse.

When Brandon's father passed, Cherish held his hand, chauffeured his ever-fussing grandmother, and volunteered to make all the arrangements. Although Madeline was there to do the same, Cherish was not so easily comforted. Even Brandon's cancer diagnosis hadn't deterred her determination to keep her flailing insides from showing up on her face. But once the complications with the brain tumor started showing up in his everyday life, she succumbed to crying spells, locking herself in the bathroom until she cried herself dry. The few weeks he had been a patient in the hospice, she watched as Cherish denied food, opting for coffee to give her stamina. To see her daughter twenty pounds lighter, her hands shaking, face drenched; Madeline could only keep her own sobs buried in the crevice of her chest, waiting for her night alone to let them roam free.

Mrs. Ollie clung to the bottom banister post. "Madeline, everything alright up there? Is Cherish okay?"

The commotion forced Tierra's eyes to pop open. Still in her "funeral dress," she had been sprawled across the bed in her grandmother's guestroom. It was the only room in the house without tales of her father's life offered up over full plates then taking a backseat to sports or politics. Basketed on the nightstand, the jasmine scented potpourri Tierra had once thought smelled too much like perfume, was a welcomed friend. As if they were her swordsmen, protecting her peace, dancing lilacs against the old cream wallpaper fought to bring light to the day of dark clouds and black suits. A day in which, I love you's meant goodbye and goodbyes meant see you soon, hopefully without tears falling from your eyes. The silky sea of the purple acetate beneath her assured not everything had changed. *Gran-Gran still loves purple. And throw pillows. Lots and lots of throw pillows.*

Shadows busying beneath the door, Tierra nestled against the longest of the six pillows. Whatever had gotten her mother riled up was going to require a mountain of energy from everyone in its path. *Better get all the rest I can. In two seconds they'll both be in here acting like whatever they've got to say is more important than the fact that Daddy isn't here.* Tierra cringed. Her eyes burned with the welling liquid. *It's not fair. He should be here.*

"Please don't go in there waking Tierra up. Stay the night. It's been a heavy day. For all of us."

Cherish was still. Her hand kept steady on the brass handle.

"Don't you think Tierra deserves a break? She's only twelve, Cherish. All this moving about from place to place with all the arrangements. How can she process it all? Give the girl a second to catch her breath. Her whole life is changing and the last thing she needs is you frantically moving about as if we're preparing for Armageddon. She passed out for Christ's sake. That's a mighty hurt she's feeling." Madeline inched toward her daughter. In the darkened corridor she could see Cherish's eyes scrambling for something to keep her focus.

Cherish rubbed her temples, but the javelin of pain would only retarget its strike. *Maybe Mommy's right. I'm being selfish. Tierra saw the moon and stars in Brandon. We haven't even made time to talk about how she's feeling. Her rose colored looking glass is being shattered. Perhaps I should give her more time to rest.*

"What's got you so worked up like this? I mean, I get your heart being in the tip of your toes. Pain swirling in your belly. But this is unlike you, racing about." Tilting her head, she rested her hand on Cherish's shoulder. "Come on back downstairs. Ollie can get the kettle going. If you like, I can ask everyone else to leave. They'll understand."

Madeline awaited her daughter's reply. She could tell Cherish was thinking. She released the door handle and sighed. Madeline exhaled. Cherish's lips pressed, her eyes glossy, she shook her head.

"My goodness, Cherish. What is it? I know this has been an ordeal, but did something happen? Someone say anything to set you off? I know Baylock can go running off at the mouth, but its all love with him. You know that, don't you?" Madeline enveloped her crying child into her bosom.

Cherish continued to shake her head. Her tongue refused to tell the story of her frustration. Her mind circled through her teenage years, Brandon's smile, and the day they brought Tierra home from the hospital. Both her fists balled, she lifted her head. Pulling herself from her mother's embrace, she proceeded with her storm into the bedroom.

Just as Tierra had been raising herself out of the bed, the door flung open. Cherish breezed through, grabbing the navy overnight bag from the corner. Tierra watched her mother rummage through the closet, collecting dresses she had worn throughout the week. Madeline stood in the threshold, her hands clasped.

Ms. Ollie had finally made it up the stairs. She squeezed past Madeline, throwing herself into the center of the room. "Cherish dear, what has come over you? This little girl doesn't need to see you acting like this. Come have a seat." Gathering Cherish up into her arms, she guided her to the rocking chair."

Tierra wondered if Ms. Ollie was a witch. The moment she sat Cherish in the rocking chair, her tears dried. She stared straight ahead.

Ms. Ollie snapped her fingers and waved her hand. "Cherish, honey, I know you're hurting but you can't shut down like this. We're all worried about you. You got your daughter here. Just as her knees buckled earlier, they'll buckle again as the weight of losing her father isn't easy for any child to carry. She can't shoulder the load without you, honey. Shouldn't have to."

Tierra listened as her mother breathed. Winded, the breaths were heavy like when she'd wear herself out chasing Tierra for a beating. As the rise and fall of her chest was slowing, Tierra tried to understand what was happening. *Is this what losing your mind looks like? Can't be. Cause I'm sure I'm losing mine and I haven't yanked any clothes out of the closet.*

Cherish's feet remained planted on the carpet. The burning glow of overexertion had dissolved. Her usual fair and freckled skin seemed porous and over-powdered under the rouge. Tierra watched as her grandmother stroked Cherish's hair, doing her best to coax her only child out of this impotence.

As if consoling a baby, Madeline spoke softly. She gave anecdotes reflecting on how Brandon was so in love with Cherish. He had always sought her strength and then tugged it out of her until she could see it herself. "If he were present, you know he'd tell you to cry today, maybe tomorrow, but then begin your healing. He was good that way, always focused on moving forward."

Madeline thought back to when Brandon and Cherish were teenagers giggling on her porch. Brandon seemed to have found a way to help

Cherish become more responsible. She'd do her chores, set the table, clean her room. Seemed she had always seen herself as his wife. From the time they met he had his sights set on college with or without sports. Cherish wasted no time adapting to his plans. Madeline had never known her to be so head over heels. She quit smoking, which Madeline and her plants was most grateful for. It was becoming a part-time job picking the butts out of the flower pots while listening to Cherish deny claim and then run through possible scenarios of how they could've gotten there. Even her bottles of holiday rum stopped going missing. Accepting her as she were, Brandon had inspired Cherish to be excited about the future. She felt safe in his presence, loved, refined and confident. But now he was gone and no amount of recalling was going to bring him back.

Madeline feared there was nothing she could do to make her child feel whole again. She knew what it was like to be a husbandless mother, even if her partner had never passed on. To have your whole life unexpectedly turned against all you planned was as frightful a detour for any woman to handle, particularly one caring for a child. The pain was staggering. Like a hundred poison-tipped arrows to the chest, the heart would bleed before it hardened. Peppered balls would rally in the throat promising not to swell if only it was agreed not to speak of the loss. Because if the soul would allow you to belt out longing cries and confess the sadness, everything would collapse and then burn.

Madeline peeked over at Tierra. Someone would need to console her. The confusion widening her eyes and stiffening her body could not be ignored. Madeline sat beside Tierra and recounted the story of when Brandon asked Madeline for Cherish's hand in marriage. "Ca-Can I ta-take you out for di-dinner tonight Ma-Mama Madeline? I-I want to talk to you a-about something." She chuckled, slapping her knee.

Tierra glanced at her mother. There was a constant in her gaze. No signs of happiness ignited; not a giggle about Brandon fumbling for his car keys nor a flinch at the repetition of his speech of undying love.

"He had this little dance of joy when he had received my blessing. You would've thought he had just won the Super Bowl."

Cherish was still in space, unmoved by the flashback. Tierra on the other hand, moved closer to Madeline. She rested her head on her shoulder, thankful for the retelling.

"Two lovebirds barely out of High School. Brandon had decided not to return to school that year. Well everyone thought he was crazy. He could've been a real football star, but that wasn't what he wanted. He wanted a simple life with my sweet Cherish." She glanced at Ollie who was gripping Cherish by the chin, inspecting her eyes. Still, no response. "His aspirations were as basic and noble as being a loving and providing husband and then an awesome Dad. Heck, once we knew Cherish was pregnant it all made sense. You know, the rush to marry. But he was over the moon with a baby on the way. The life he always dreamed of." She grinned at Tierra as she smoothed the restless strands of the girl's hair. Letting out the deepest of sighs, she continued, "I couldn't deny him that. Cherish was his universe and you could see that he was completely fulfilled, knowing she'd have him and a child for him to call his own. It was a good life. That's how he'd tell it. His family was his golden coin."

Ms. Ollie interjected. "I think it would be best if Tierra stayed with you for a little while, Maddy. Cherish can't care for her like this."

Panic scurried through Tierra's veins. Wasn't her mother was just having a hard moment? Why was everyone in such a rush to push her past it? Her dad had just been been lowered into the ground with shovel of dirt piled on top of him, no one was going to be okay today. Not her mother, not her. "Mommy doesn't have to care for me. I can care for her. She needs me."

Finally breaking her glare, Cherish looked over at Tierra. Her face moist with dripping tears, she shook her head.

"Mommy, no! What are you saying," Tierra shouted. She was compelled to run, but with all the people downstairs, she believed there'd be nowhere to hide. "Why are you doing this," she sobbed. "We need each other. You can't leave me alone like this."

Madeline pulled Tierra into her bosom. She rocked her back and forth as the girl's cries dampened her breasts. "Long as I'm here you will never be alone. Okay baby? Just give your mother some time." She peeked at Cherish who was nodding her agreement. "We'll get through this together, giving each other what we need. No one's doing this alone. I promise."

Cherish wiped her face dry. She stood, still clutching her garments. Quietly she packed them in her bag. She kissed her mother's cheek then Tierra's crown. With Tierra's snivels rhythming her steps, Cherish made her way out of the room. She wouldn't look back.

5 IN THE LAND OF CADEN

After locking themselves back in their dorm room, Tierra and Michelle positioned themselves Indian style in the middle of the blood colored rug at the center of the floor. Its plush reminded Tierra of the bear rugs she imagined were stretched across the living rooms of every wealthy person ever. It matched Michelle's bed ensemble.

"You actually walk with your own carpeting," Michelle mocked.

Both girls doubled over with laughter.

"Remember you asked me that? I knew I liked you then. You seemed quiet, thoughtful maybe, but you weren't intimidated. Michelle adjusted her breasts. "I know what living with a rack like this can do to a neighbor's self-esteem."

Before rooming with Michelle, Tierra had never seen fake boobs, but the moment she met Michelle she was sure hers weren't real. They filled her studded tank top to capacity and seemed like if you touched them they'd squeak like a balloon on the edge of bursting. *Gotta admit, they are nice. If I were a boy I'd be chasing her little ass too. But mine aren't so bad are they?* The peered down her shirt.

Michelle poured pineapple vodka into a blue plastic cup, filling it a quarter of the way. Then adding Moscato, she gently swirled the cup around. "Smells good." She passed the cup to Tierra.

Tierra paused. She studied the dangling cup. *Of all the times to be a cliché; first sip of alcohol is under peer pressure during my freshman year in college.* So far, college had been nothing like she expected. Sure, she was free from ten o'clock curfews and rooster early Sunday mornings, but she wondered what the point of freedom was if she wasn't going to use it to make dumb kid choices like everyone else in the world. Everyone around her appeared to be having the time of his or her lives while she bustled from class to class desperate to make a scholarly impression, secretly trying to chase away what might be her tendency to repeat her mother's mistakes. *But who am I becoming? Definitely not anyone people would notice. Why do I have to be sentenced to obscurity because of Mommy was a mommy before her time?* "You know, what? Give it here."

Michelle obliged then poured another for herself. "The key is not to drink it too quickly. If you toss it back, you'll be dazed and dumb for the rest of the..." Tierra had already downed the contents of her cup. She was licking the rim for additional drops. Michelle dipped her head to get a look at Tierra's eyes. "Girl, you might just be better than me at holding liquor. That was like eight ounces you just threw back like a shot. You're not even cross-eyed."

"It tastes like punch." Tierra shrugged then held her cup out, awaiting the next serving. The liquid warmed in her chest, going down much smoother than she expected. Noting the immediate rise in her temperature, she anxiously stared at Michelle sipping her own. "Um, hello!"

Excitedly, Tierra watched as Michelle refilled her empty vessel. "You know, I'm really not a prude. It's just I feel so out of place all the time. You're the only friend I've made since I've been here. No one's interested in who I am so it feels awkward to try to get to know anyone. Everyone seems to be problem free and I'm still reckoning the tattered map of my home life. I thought being away from home would feel much more… I don't know, liberating."

"My mom sent me away to school and camps practically my entire life. You feel out of place here because you felt like you belonged somewhere else, probably with your dad. He's the only person I hear you really talk about and I know he passed away. Don't worry though. You're privileged to have belonged somewhere, to someone for some time."

Tierra contemplated Michelle's words as she finished off her drink. She relished the mixture of the fruity bitterness dancing on her tongue. Maybe she should just accept the blessing her dad was and try to move on from mourning him. *But how could I when my mother won't talk about him or talk to me if I bring up his name?*

There was a knock at the door. Michelle jumped to answer it. She checked the time on her diamond-faced watch. "Shoot, I didn't think it was this late. I gotta get dressed for work."

Attempting to move as abruptly as Michelle had leapt, Tierra's head felt light and her vision blurred. *Well, I think I'm buzzed.* She re-steadied herself on the floor. As Michelle was greeting the visitor, Tierra's thoughts started to race. *What if it's a serial killer at the door? But then we're in a dorm with 200 other girls. Would someone be so bold? And they did knock so unless that's their thing, it might not be a murderer. Oh, but what if it is?*

As if reading the panic of her mind, Michelle called out, "It's Caden!"

Tierra furrowed her brows. "Who the hell is Caden?" *Did she invite those guys we saw at the liquor store back to the room? Oh my God, that voice sounds really manly. And I've been drinking. Okay it's not security because she knows him, right? Just be cool and everything will be fine.* She surveyed the room for something to defend herself with in case she was wrong. Quickly, she reached for the ruler from her desk. With her limbs lacking sober coordination, she toppled over her folded legs. Meanwhile Michelle had let *Caden* in.

Struggling with an ill attempt at pulling herself together, Tierra looked up and saw what she could only compare to the gleam of heaven finally having mercy on her. *Caden. Caden, what a beautiful man, and name, and oh my Lord. Such splendor in his toothy smile. Bye-bye, Mr. Leonard.*

A six-foot-four cherry chocolate man with broad shoulders and dazzling chestnut eyes looked down on her. Her heart had somehow grown flapping wings and was running about in her chest. Her cheeks flushed. The warmth that settled in her belly woke again, travelling in tingles to her fingers and toes. She hadn't realized she was still bent over after brushing her knees until his voice carried her out of her daze.

"Need help?"

Tierra took his hand and allowed him to help her stand. She was sure her grin was wider that appropriate. The aches in her cheeks told her so.

"Caden, this is Tierra, roommate and friend. Can't forget friend. She's sensitive. Now everyone knows everyone." In a hurry, Michelle stuffed stringed underwear and beads into a bag with an oversized makeup pouch. Answering what she believed was the room's impending question, "Yes, I'm going to jump in the shower real quick. I'm not a funk box, you know. Crap, where are my yellow stilettos?"

Caden had not looked away. Tierra didn't want him to. There was a man standing before her and if she kept still long enough, then maybe, he'd take her for a woman. He smelled like one of the vials of oil the man with the Kufi hat used to try to sell her grandmother's friend, Mr. Baylock, when Tierra would accompany him to the supermarket.

In silence she stared at his beauty, hoping to someday take possession. Time, however, was nudging Tierra to move along when she realized Michelle was already returning from her shower. "So, you're uh, Michelle's um…"

"Brother. Well, sort of. My father, her mom, anyway, I work the door at Lucy's."

Michelle chimed in. "Now see you blew your chance, Caden. Talking about Lucy's," she scoffed. "Tierra here thinks a place like that is beneath her and she wouldn't be caught dead there. She calls it a strip-club, no matter how many times I tell her we are an established gentlemen's club. And here you go telling her you guard the entryway to hell."

Tierra smiled shyly. "I never said that. As a matter of fact, if you don't mind, Caden, I'd like to ride you, I mean, ride with you guys down there. I'm kind of curious about the place my beloved roommate emerges from with glitter in her hair yet not enough energy to give a full yawn in the mornings."

"Don't let this one pressure you," Caden warned. "She does that. Lucy's ain't for everyone. I don't mind if you want to roll with us, though." His grin was a knowing one, keeping her secret of just wanting to bask in his presence. "I think it's cute that you've never been. Mostly everyone that goes here has."

Michelle smirked as she stepped out into the hallway. "Yup, cute. That's a good word for it. I don't think anyone has ever called me cute for working there though. Maybe I should ask one of my clients tonight if he thinks I'm cute."

Determined not to be left behind, Tierra grabbed her leather jacket (the most fashionable garment she owned). She hurried behind them. "Michelle, you've been begging me to come see you perform for the longest. So now I'm coming." She glanced at Caden. Her grandmother's spiel echoed in her head. *Don't think I'm letting you live on campus so you can go out there chasing every damn boy you lay your eyes on. I'm not stupid. I know at your age and with your good looks you'll attract male attention. Just don't go throwing yourself at every man's foot. Make them believe you're not thinking about them. Let them do the chasing.*

Caden held the back door of his SUV open for Tierra. He held her hand as she stepped inside. Once she was buckled in, he winked before closing the door.

Michelle rolled her eyes as she seated herself in the front passenger. "Oh boy. Don't you two go making my life awkward now."

6 TOO MUCH TALK

Michelle had one foot comfortably up on the dashboard. From the backseat, Tierra stared at the olive toned beauty, curious. Michelle had made passing mention of her African and Asian ethnicity as if it were a blessing bestowed upon birth, but now, drowning in the tunes of a *Quiet Storm* station, she wondered if Michelle's confidence was more recently contrived at the start of her employment with Lucy's. *I mean I guess men pouring money over you, basically praising your body would make anyone feel confident, right? But she acts like she's a budding moving star. She does have a great body, though. She's certainly got the right breast for her profession. I wonder how much she paid for them.*

As they rode past neighborhoods unfamiliar to Tierra, it occurred to her that she would've never been able to locate anything that wasn't within a mile from the campus. Michelle had a car and a year of college under her belt, but still she seemed to know how to get around the city much easier than Tierra would. *You know I never asked her if she's from around here.* They talked about the schools Michelle had attended throughout High School but never where her mother or her several daddy stand-ins were settled.

My roommate's a stripper, her brother or her sort of brother happens to live in the same town she goes to school in, and he's a bouncer at the club where she works? You're an ass, Tierra! Of course she's from around here. She's familiar with damn near every place we've ever been. Still though, she'd be sent away for school all her life and then go local for college? And why does she live in the dorm. Well that I can actually understand. There's no way her mom would let her live like she does, taking her clothes off for a living and what not. Right? Wait, why does this even matter to me? I swear my grandmother has her nosey remnants all over me.

As the car slowed, a long pink and green neon sign hanging at the side of what looked to be a warehouse became legible. Above the silhouette of a naked woman luxuriating in an oversized martini glass, the sign read, *LUCY'S*. The letters took turns blinking.

Caden turned his car into the parking lot. Tierra's spine tingled. She watched as they drove past the winding line leading to the front door. Countless men. Some Tierra thought she recognized from a few of her classes. A number of the older men she thought should be home reading bedtime stories to their grandchildren. Still, she was awestruck at the consistent swelling of the crowd. *This is what I always thought nightclubs to be like, but I thought it was just a childish exaggeration of what I'd seen on television. It's actually true. Holy crap!* Some of the waiting women were casually dressed in boots and jeans. Then there were some whose outfits could've competed with the night's dancers. *Oh my God! What if it's Amateur Night? That would be crazy. I wonder if I could do it.* Following behind Caden and Michelle, she glided through the back door. Tierra shrieked. *Okay, we get the celebrity treatment. This is kind of awesome!*

Caden, now on duty, backed out and darted around to the front, helping to oversee the club's entrance. Michelle led Tierra through the dressing room and out onto into what was dubbed, "The Great Room."

"It's Thursday night. We call it, "Thirsty Night," for all the patrons who showed for the ten-dollar lap dances. Every other night lap dances are twenty." Women bustled through the hallways calling out table numbers. Michelle explained, "We look out for each other. Tell each other which tables are spending."

The temperature in the dressing room was hotter than Georgia in July. Fog traveled throughout. A party bowl of scents crept through Tierra's nostrils; perfume, baby wipes, powder, lubricant, spilled alcohol, *and a burnt skunk? Please tell me no one's privates' smell like skunk. That's just nasty!*

Women sitting against a wall catty-corner from the bathroom, dumped tobacco into candy store paper bags, re-rolling the cigars with droppings from tiny Ziplocs. Cheshire Cat-like smiles, they motioned for Tierra to join. Her decline was met with shrugs, pulls of smoke, and heads leaned back with half shut eyelids. They appeared to inhale in slow motion, savoring every pull, every puff, blowing the winds of released burdens. Their chortles quieted. Tierra continued to eye the women peripherally; afraid they'd take offense to her staring. *I wonder what that feels like.* When there was nothing left to pass, instinctively they all rose ready to get to work.

Some of the other women carried their heads like dainty ballerinas or queens passing crowds of their subjects. Tierra admired the ease in which they could be seen as business savvy, commanding their own means, counting their earned ends.

A few others stood. Some squatted, posing in front of the floor length mirrors that leaned against the bubble gum pink wallpaper. Tierra counted a dozen in the row. No one sat at the few vanity stations available. They were merely places to stock make-up, see facial details, and add hairpieces.

As she dressed, Michelle talked over her shoulder. "The owner, Mr. Cherry thinks that chairs make the dancers lazy. Standing, squatting, it firms the calves, toughens the thighs. Keeps us appealing, he says. Weird I know, but he's kind of right. My legs never looked so good until I started working here last summer."

So that's how she keeps her legs like that? Dang, I need to start squatting. I could use some muscle to hold up this butt of mine.

Mr. Cherry turned from the corner in which he collected dollars. Immediately he zoned in on Tierra. He was a slender built, brown-skinned, leather-faced man. Taken aback, by his presence Tierra mused, *By God, this man is the antidote to the legend, 'Black don't crack.' Daaamn! Dude 'bout to mess up our reputation with his tougher than leather skin.*

"Hey Mr. Cherry. This is my friend Tierra."

The woman Mr. Cherry was collecting from kissed his cheek and hurried out of the dressing room. Her breasts covered in a metallic string bikini top, bounced in rhythm of her trot. Mr. Cherry watched the woman's exposed bottom as it too jiggled. Tierra gave the man a once-over, looking to identify what about him was so extraordinary. *Whatever it is, must be a some secret society kind of secret.*

Diamond-rimmed oversized glasses, Mr. Cherry, swaggered like every woman in his establishment was there for his eyes only. A red crushed velvet jacket was casually unbuttoned atop his black collar shirt, which was tucked into his black trousers. The top two buttons on his shirt were unfastened to allow his black and white polka dot ascot to be on full display. He kept a toothpick lodged at the side of his mouth as he spoke.

"Nice! You dance?" Mr. Cherry looked down at Tierra's calves then huffed. "No, you ain't no dancer. If you are, you've been working at the wrong place for far too long." He circled Tierra, leering at her breasts, then her thighs, taking pause when catching sight of her behind.

Mr. Cherry fancied himself as having a keen eye for talent. It was evident this young woman was a newcomer, but her ability to entice wouldn't take much to hone. Hazel eyes, thick tresses, stacked bottom, he envisioned the dollars pouring in. He knew if he were attracted, then with a little make-up and a lot less clothing, the customers would also be enthralled. His blood juiced and his mind flooded with pictures of what she'd look like winding the stages poles. He adjusted his belt, doing little to mask his body's excitement.

"She's just looking around." Michelle tried diverting Mr. Cherry's impending offer. She had just wanted Tierra to have a good time, step outside of herself for once. Not pressure her into becoming a dancer. The girl had been the model student since she arrived but it was clear she was dying a slow mundane death. She just wanted to give Tierra an avenue to help her have fun for the night, not change how she lived.

Tierra was still scrutinizing Mr. Cherry's assumptions. *Who the hell is he to say I'm not a dancer? How does he know? Taking inventory of my body like that with his old ass. These cratered faces haven't got anything on me. Michelle's cute, but she's like the best looking one in here. Well maybe the chick over there in ostrich feathers. She's kind of pretty. Okay yes some of them have some incredible bodies, but still I could be a dancer. My tummy may not have a six-pack and all but it's flat. Yes, my behind is big, but last I checked women be injecting all kinds of foolishness into their butts to get it to look like mine. And what I got is au-natural! This frail, old, trying to be a player, creep got some nerve!*

"I was looking around to see what the big deal was," Tierra finally answered. Her pulse was racing. It was too late to retract. *Might as well play up this façade. This man ain't gonna make me feel like some naïve, flabby, little reject who's less than him or anyone else.*

Intrigued, Mr. Cherry scoffed. "Well you go ahead and check us out then, Miss Tierra! Actually, we'd appreciate it if you gave us the same opportunity to check you out. Grace us with your presence on stage and let's see if you know how to generate money. You're a bit overdressed, your makeup understated (if you even have on any) and I understand you probably didn't bring a costume with you, but I'm sure you're not too shy to dance as you came. Not a brave girl like you with all that attitude."

Tierra had said too much. *Wait, what? Is he joking? Did I just talk myself into a stripper's audition? Excuse me, exotic dancer. Still, I can't. But everyone's going to laugh at me if I don't, so... I mean I did just... Did just what? Totally misrepresent myself? I'm probably embarrassing the hell out of Michelle. What if she tells Caden about this? But it's just dancing, right? So, I do a little moving, blow a few kisses, and embarrass myself in my panties. At least I'd have a funny story to tell my grandchildren one day.*

Michelle watched as Tierra's head titled. *Get the freak out of town! She's actually considering it.* She giggled. *This girl is full of surprises. Well, I hope her nerves are stronger than the girl who came in here showing her ass last week. She threw up all over those cute little shoes. Tierra should know she doesn't need to do this for my benefit, right? She doesn't need to impress me. But what am I talking about? Maybe she's got a little rude gal in her and she's enlightening me. Let her go ahead. This is probably the most daring thing she's done her whole life.*

With all the false confidence she could muster, Tierra addressed Mr. Cherry, slowly strutting toward him as she spoke. "Money's not the issue so please don't pretend that it is. I'll tell you what; instead of me going to dance on the stage, how about I dance for you? Here, privately. That's what you really want, isn't it?"

The dressing room erupted with catcalls and a number of, "You go girl," and "Well," in support of a private showing. Tierra appreciated the encouragement. If only it could alleviate the nervous tickle swirling her bladder.

"All right. Settle down everyone. I admire your boldness, Miss Tierra. It's certainly not an offer I get every day."

Someone yelled, "Awe, Mr. Cherry you were killing them back in your day." The dancers laughed.

"Yes, I know, very funny. Okay, Miss Tierra, you can dance for me, but we don't need much privacy, as you say. You can dance for us all, right now. Give all these professionals a real show."

Tierra saw the only way for her to have the last word in this confrontation was to merely accept Mr. Cherry's challenge. He had to know that she wasn't just some little girl visiting with her, "Aunt Michelle." She was grown and just as desirable as any of the other women he had dancing for him. More importantly, she deserved his respect.

As the room quieted, Tierra began to feel intimidated. *Mommy obviously did much more than this when she was my age. So no biggie. Look, I'll take the drink this waitress is offering. She probably knows I'm my nipples are frightened.* She tossed back two shot glasses of a brown liquor. The liquid glided down her throat. But the rush to her head, that was the jolt she was searching for.

One of the bathroom smokers docked her iPod into a set of speakers. Tierra expected to hear a thumping base and fast paced Southern rapping or some wild rock song about being free. However, the slow croons of an R&B singer was something she'd need to take her time with. She couldn't just bounce and shake like a YouTube challenge. No, this would require eyes closed, transportation into her imagination, like when she was alone in her dorm room fantasizing about Mr. Leonard.

Tierra swayed to her left, then to her right. Off-beat at first, but then finding her sync with the rhythm, she flowed. In full control, slowly she spun her hips like webbing for prey. Hugging her parted thighs with every move, her jeans clung to her fullness, yielding the hunger for seduction. She had become one with the sultry serenade. She swung her extended brunette tresses from side to side, surging the allurement. Her arms moved like the conductors of her motions. Her breasts chose their own cadence in line with the offering. She became the lyrics blaring from the speakers,

"…Seductively courageous: She makes believers of the faithless."

While she danced, the blackness of pressed eyes allowed her to relax, guided by the music. There were no outer thoughts, no worries, and no judges. If she could only keep them closed until she made it outside, into the back of Caden's car, until she was tucked away safe in her bed.

The sultry melody died down into a faded whisper. *This is like the dreams of being naked in public except you realize you fell asleep in front of the whole student body and they're all watching for the moment you awaken.*

Fueled by the memory of her grandmother's advice before her small role in a school play, *You better own it or they will laugh you out of here,* Tierra opened her eyes. Everyone was staring, jaws dropped. Tierra took up a space next to Michelle and folded her arms. Despite what Mr. Cherry would say, she felt good. Michelle was smiling.

"Someone get this girl a chair," Mr. Cherry demanded. "That was phenomenal. When can you start?"

Okay what just happened? I can't dance here. My grandmother would kill me. It did feel good, but... Gosh, can you imagine if I was on stage? I probably could've gotten a whole bunch of money. Maybe I don't have to answer right now. I'll call and say no tomorrow. I'm just going to have fun tonight.

7 A DIFFERENT SPRING

Late March. Spring was just airing its scent among the trees. A young Cherish had just lined her mother's potted daffodils along the porch railing. Pleased with her effort, she took a seat on the stoop.

Each car that zoomed by yanked at Cherish's heart. Brandon had already warned her that the practice schedule wouldn't allow for him to come home for Spring Break. Still she hoped. At the sight of the broad shouldered young man walking the sidewalk toward her house, Cherish leapt. The royal blue football jacket, identical to Brandon's was all she could make out so far up the street; a later reminder that she should wear her contacts even when just lounging around the house. For now, she believed that indeed her prayer for his homecoming had been answered.

However, as the figure grew closer, she could see the young man's complexion was clearly darker. She then noticed the twisted tresses that hung to the gentleman's shoulder. As he passed her stoop she spoke his name. "Jackson?"

Jackson paused his stroll. He turned to find the breathtaking girl he had only met once before, hair wrapped in a scarf, face emulating the sun. "Cherish? Wow, I hadn't anticipated seeing you."

She drew in her breath. His smile was brighter than she remembered. His teeth pronounced but well maintained. Skin milky dark like the sweetest of chocolates. "You remember my name."

"You're pretty unforgettable." He invited himself to sit beside her. "You live here?"

"Nah, just kickin' it on a random stoop."

Immediately Jackson pulled himself up.

Cherish chuckled. "Stupid question gets a stupid answer. Yeah, I do. You think I'm just combing the city for stoops to trespass?" She was eager to hear his laugh.

He obliged, but then quickly hushed.

Cherish searched her mind for something to say. "So why are you walking my block exactly?"

Again, he offered his grin. "My cousin Lanaeya lives down the road in the corner house. We grew up like siblings since we're both only children. The spring breaks when I don't visit, she visits me. Surprised I've never seen you through the years."

Cherish thought about past spring vacations from school. She was usually on punishment for something reported by a church elder like when she got caught choking on a cigarette in the boy's bathroom. *Probably best not to bring that up.* Her life had taken a contrary twist since she met Brandon. She wasn't the girl behind bathroom stall scribbles nor the one to be hid from mothers anymore.

"Wait. I thought you guys had practice."

Jackson bit his lip. He kept his eyes on the people who trotted past them. He sighed.

Cherish scowled, waiting for an explanation. She was sure if Jackson could be excused from practice then Brandon very well should be home too. "Is there practice?" She was afraid to hear the answer, but had to hear it nonetheless. Her mind circled in a panic. Aligning Brandon with any type of falsehood was something she never would've fathomed.

Again, Jackson let out a deep breath. "Practice starts on Wednesday. Coach let us have the weekend and a couple days break." Immediately he turned to Cherish to ease the confusion he imagined her to have. "If Brandon told you he couldn't come home because of practice, believe him. He loves you a great deal and I can almost guarantee you that he's not with someone else."

Cherish's face reddened. "Someone else? Why would you say that?"

It was his turn to panic. "I didn't mean to insinuate, I just meant... Well isn't that what girls worry about?"

Still flustered, but regaining her calm, Cherish answered, "I guess. Most other girls anyway."

"Look, don't think about it. We were just here having a peaceful take of the good weather. This is my fault. I interrupted your good mood..."

"With what? Walking down the street? This is Brandon's fault for not being honest with me. What's he doing if he's not practicing? He hasn't answered my calls from this morning."

Jackson got up. He dusted the seat of his pants. "I don't want to be a wedge between you and Brandon. He knows he'd be a fool to hurt you so I doubt he would. He's just not that kind of guy. I don't know what he's doing, but I should be leaving."

Before she knew what she was doing, Cherish had tugged on Jackson's arm. "Stay." The electricity that flowed through her fingers tempered her grip. Quickly, she drew her hand back. "I'm sorry."

Daring to look into Cherish's eyes, Jackson nodded. "I want to." He took his seat beside her. In silence they tried watching the trees sway, the flowers attempt to bloom, the leaves scatter the sidewalk. Each of them had mind to tell the other that Jackson shouldn't stay. Neither of them, though, had the will to part.

8 OUT OR INTO THE DARK

Thanksgiving break seemed to come much quicker than Tierra expected. Countless nights after her "audition" she'd lay awake, imagining what it'd be like to fully enter the world or exotic dancing. *Would I use my real name? I wonder if they get to pick their own songs. How would I tell Gran she didn't need to pay for college anymore? I'm sure I could make enough to afford it myself.* She chuckled at the fantasticness of the fantasy every night before falling asleep. *Who am I kidding? Cherish Proper would have a heart attack and Gran would lay me in the grave right next to her.*

In her grandmother's living room, Tierra sat on the sofa, legs folded beneath her. Out of the oversized window, she watched as the wind blew dustings from the snow piles. This year's snowfall had come early. She had never experienced a white Thanksgiving. *I wonder if this is*

God's idea of a joke. All them years of praying for a white Christmas.

Neighborhood kids appreciated the anomaly. Bundled in their puffy coats and bright colored scarves, they built snowmen and tossed snowballs while their parents stood on porches, sipping from coffee tumblers. The hard-plastic sofa covering was slow to detach from her thighs when she shifted her body weight. Accustomed to the pull, she grabbed the crocheted blanket from the couch's back to rest her legs on while she continued to admire the children playing.

For Tierra, Thanksgiving proved to be as boring and uneventful as they had over the past five years. She and her grandmother did the regular assertions of what they were thankful for, which agitated Tierra. With Cherish was seated in the recliner, perusing her own thoughts and giving little more than a nod of agreement, listing blessings seemed contradictory. From time to time, Tierra would catch her mother's glare. Once she thought she detected a smile, but figured it was better to not make a to-do out of it. The woman never said anything that wasn't a generality, if she spoke at all. Tierra tired of needing her mother's attention.

"Tierra." Her grandmother called from the kitchen. She thought to yell back but then considered her grandmother's repetitive lecture, *When I call you, come.*

Entering the kitchen, Tierra found her grandmother seated at the table. The woman seemed older than just yesterday, her wiry silver hair sweeping her shoulders. She was hunched over a spread of the day's mail. "You okay Gran?"

"Yes, baby. Have a seat." Madeline patted the cushion of the chair next to hers. "I've got a little extra money and I wanted to make sure you have some for your pocket. You're doing wonderfully away at that school." She patted Tierra's hand. "So, so proud of you."

As her grandmother wrote out a check for five hundred dollars, Tierra noticed an envelope addressed to her. "Gran, why does this have my name on it? And why has it already been torn open?" She flipped the envelope over to find the sender listed as, Mr. Jackson Trent.

Madeline bit her lip.

"Gran? Wait, is this the Jackson Trent who my father used to talk about? The football player who he went to college with?"

Madeline nodded. She kept her eyes focused on the check, but her hand decided it no longer wanted to keep writing.
Tierra brushed aside additional papers scattered across the kitchen table. One looked to be a handwritten letter. She held it up, quickly reading through its contents.

Madeline sighed as she listened to Tierra read.

"Weird that I've never met you, I know, but please understand that just knowing you exist,

I love you. Your grandmother has been kind enough to send me updates on your well-being and I keep your graduation picture in my wallet. If you ever need anything, please never hesitate to ask." Her face was growing red with fury. "My loving father? Gran, what is this guy talking about? Brandon is my father and why would you take this guy's money and send him my picture?" She slammed the letter on the table.

Madeline sprung from her chair. "Wait a doggone minute now, Tierra. I get that this distresses you, but don't you for one second think I'm going to let you change your stripes and start screaming at me. Now you pull yourself together and settle your tone so I can explain."

9 FATHER TO FATHER

A dark and frigid night, the sea of cars in the parking lot of Pathway Hospice was thinning. Shivering, Brandon sat alone with the engine running. His co-workers had all waved their goodbyes, the last of which took off twenty minutes ago.

This is the lot it, he thought. He recalled the doctor's prognosis. *You may experience bouts of numbness, sensitivity to cold. We'll do everything we can, but... Where the infection is located in the brain and then of course the size of the tumor... I don't want to give you false hope.*

Several times throughout the past few months he felt his body parts tingling before falling limp. Eleven days ago, it happened while he was driving down Howard Avenue. Thankfully, the car had only tapped the curb before stopping. A congregation of young men shooting dice in front of Pop's Corner Store heard the collision. One ran over to ensure he was okay. Another stepped around to inspect his car. Two more shuffled over and assisted him out of the car. He was grateful for their concern. And the beer. The ease of their chatter led him to reveal his condition.

"Man, we need to call your wife then. You gotta tell her what happened."

Brandon chuckled. The young man sounded like the men at his mother-in-law's church. Always pushing to get the wife involved. Senior men with more years of marriage than he had accumulated in life.

"Whenever I get into something and my girl ain't the first to know…"

"Yeah my moms still be flipping on my pops and they not even together. They weird, man. You should lead with telling her you're not hurt though. My mom always says lead with the that first."

Brandon heeded to the urging. It was during that call that he was realized it was time to accept that he needed to give the hospice his two-week notice. However, it was his failing memory and sleepless nights that warned there was someone else he'd need to make aware.

As he shifted the gear into drive, Brandon's cell phone began to vibrate. He peered at the dashboard. Earlier that morning he dialed the same area code appearing across the screen. Knowing he'd need to take the call in Cherish's absence, he threw the gear back into park and answered.

"Brandon Proper here."

"Hey Brandon! Blast from the past. I'm not even going to ask how you got my number. Jackson chuckled. "What's up, man? My assistant gave me your message. How's life treating you? It's been over ten years."

Brandon bit the insides of his cheeks. For days he had planned his words. He turned them around in his head. Then watched them fade as he pictured his wife's fury had she known what he intended to reveal.

"Hello? You still there?"

I should get on with it. "Life has treated me pretty well for many years, Jackson. Unfortunately, now I must give it it's due."

"What in the.. Man you're messing with me. Been reading too much Shakespeare or something there, buddy. You sure you're feeling alright?" Jackson's chortle was unsure.

Brandon stared out of his window. Flakes of snow began to fall. He watched as they touched the ground, each seeming to dissolve. "I'm sorry. This shouldn't be your burden, but here I am about to make it so."

"What's going on, guy? You in some kind of trouble?"

As if they too were waiting to hear his words, the flakes stopped falling as quickly as they started. No longer could he hear the rattling of his keys as the heat gusted against them. "I'm dying. Cancer. Was in the pancreas a while. Metastasized. Messing around in my brain now. Today I'm lucid, but tomorrow, who knows?"

"Oh wow, I'm sorry to hear that. I'd ask if you've tried everything, but my guess is you have. Unless that's why you're calling. I's be happy to make a few phone calls…"

"Before you go trying to save me, hear me out. Because I've accepted what's to come for me. Now's the time to get all affairs in order. Clear old debts so to speak. No matter how difficult… or painful. So please, just listen."

"You got it, man."

"My wife, Cherish, is a good woman. Not perfect, but good. Never could keep a secret from me. It'd roll off her tongue like a tumbleweed the moment she opened her mouth. Been like that since the day I met her. Anyway, what I'm getting at is…"

"Brandon, look I…"

Brandon interjected, "You promised." He needed the silence to keep track of his words. The clutter of overlapping apologies and the anger he knew would come, would mangle his thoughts.

Jackson paused.

"I know about you and Cherish. Yes, but that's not entirely the purpose of my call." Brandon took a deep breath. He'd have to be quick with what was to come. Jackson's silence couldn't be expected to continue much longer.

"Told me back then, all those years ago. And yes, I married her anyway. I believed she made a mistake. An easy one given your popularity and charisma at the time. But I never felt I could live without her. Never wanted to."

"You were like an angel on water in her eyes."

"And she in mine. However, that bond gave us little room for the rest of the world. We chose it over everything, despite how wrong we were."

A vibration called his attention to the dash. Cherish was calling on the other line. By now she had already called the security desk, inquiring if he'd left yet. She knew that it took exactly twelve minutes for him to drive home. She'd estimate time for him to warm the car, but wouldn't let too much time pass before needing to know that he was alright. However, Brandon decided to let the call go to voicemail.

"Dying puts the sins you forgot into perspective and then lines them in the front row for you to get a good look." Brandon turns his words over on his tongue. None of them tasted good. "My daughter, our daughter, Tierra; she's twelve. I won't insult you by doing the math for you." He listens to the anticipated breathing on the other end.

Jackson felt his heart stop. His mind rotated Brandon's sentence. He turned it upside down, doing his own math. "So, you mean to tell me I have a family?"

"A daughter."

"Un-freaking-believable! What is this to you? A joke?"

Brandon could hear the thud of blunt objects against Jackson's walls. He imagined the football player to be in his hotel room, preparing for tomorrow's game. Had he thought it through he might've called weeks ago, giving him much more time to process before Christmas. And what about Christmas for Tierra? Would Jackson be able to keep his distance? She was only twelve and Brandon's failing health was becoming harder to keep secret from her. She'd ask questions, demanding answers then pursing her lips at the weak tales he and Cherish would concoct.

"Twelve years without my family, Brandon! And you're only telling me because you're convinced you're about to check out. So what if you don't die? Not that I care at this point. Actually, I'd prefer you go to hell!"

Brandon held his head. Jackson's shouting was piercing his inner ear then sending the pain around to the back of his skull. Nausea swirled with regret encaged in his chest. *Perhaps I should've taken this to my death.*

"What I could've done with twelve years." Tremors in his Jackson's voice struggled to wall the tears eager to stream down his face. "You stole her from me. And now in your last hours you want forgiveness. Won't get that here, my brother! What am I supposed to do? She doesn't know me. Does she even know *about* me? Did you tell her?"

"No. I'll leave that to Cherish if she chooses."

"Again, with what Cherish chooses. The two of you just making all the decisions. Doesn't matter whose life or love is at hand. Long as the two of you are happy. And what do I do, twiddle my thumbs? I'm sure I could take you to court, but a child who doesn't know me won't want to know me after that. So, what am I left with Brandon? What the hell did you call for?"

Brandon checked the time on the dashboard. It was after eleven. It wouldn't be long before Cherish called again, worrying if he had another "incident." He put the car in drive. Another glance over at the phone screen revealed Jackson had ended their call.

At the first red light, Brandon tapped open the bottle of medicinal marijuana pills he scored from a supplier he found on the Internet. His doctors hadn't advised he take them, but they were successful in tempering his pain. If his timing was correct, they'd kick in about the time he was parking in front of the house. He laughed. *Timing hasn't been my thing lately, has it?* He kept the pill in his hand and tossed the bottle onto the passenger seat. *I'll take it soon as I'm in front of the house.*

A dancing melody played over his speaker as his cell phone buzzed. Jackson's number appeared once again. Brandon hesitated. *Jackson was correct in his fury but the screaming might impede my ability to concentrate on the road.* The melody stopped then started up again. *Maybe I'm just trying to run from this. I can't. Not anymore.* He answers.

His tone calm Jackson repeated his question, "What was it that you wanted from me?"

Brandon sighed. "First, we don't want any money from you. Cherish doesn't even know I'm telling you all of this. However, if Tierra ever found out and decided to come find you, I'd ask that you welcome her into your heart and not turn her away. Her grandfather passed on a few years ago and there aren't many men in her life. If she ever has to unhinge this web, I pray you don't reject her."

"Reject her? My own child? So you're telling me to act like she doesn't exist until she says she seeks me? *If* she does?" Jackson scoffed. "You know what? Your balls are as big as Kilimanjaro.

But, you're dying right? Nothing to be afraid of except being locked out of heaven. Now you get to go to the pearly gates with a cleared conscious. Fuck me! Thanks for calling!"

10 THINGS CHANGE PEOPLE

Dragging her suitcase, Tierra entered her dorm room. Michelle was sitting atop her comforter with her laptop set over her folded knees. *How does she love pink and red so much? It's like every day is Valentine's Day.*

From the blaring television, women shouted insults at each other. The crowd egging them on, the women then fought while they wore their wedding dresses. Michelle chortled despite never raising her head from her laptop. *And this girl makes B's. Look at her. I bet she's not doing anything related to school. Probably online shopping.*

Michelle danced four nights a week. Every time she had a paper due, she'd get on her laptop and turn on everything violent. Whenever Tierra would look over her shoulder, she'd be on a page displaying the items in her shopping cart. Michelle would hop on the defense. *Mind your business. I'll get my work done. Don't be over there judging me. Not everyone has a grandmother to teach us how to properly prepare for the world and be an "intellectual young lady."*

Tierra tried to shake the echoes of her grandmother's advice. Several times she heard herself repeat them to Michelle. *"Poor preparation leads to piss poor performance!"* However, tonight it was of no concern to her. She felt betrayed by her grandmother's secret conversations with Jackson. *Why would she let that bastard tear our family apart like this? For God's sake my freaking mother basically stopped talking behind catching wind that he might come looking for me. No one wanted to touch that though, right? "Hey Tierra, FYI it's not you. Your mother just saw a man claiming to be your father announce on television that he was retiring to spend time with his daughter. It so happened to be the day we laid your father to rest, so you know she's not really crazy, just dealing with a bunch of skeletons doing backflips out of the freaking closet." No, that's too much of an explanation. You know us children are better off with lies. My father loved Gran and she's just willing to take this Jackson guy's word? How does she know my dad really called him? And why is he so willing to pay for me to go to school? I need a damn drink. I know Michelle has got to have something somewhere around here.*

Entranced by her thoughts, Tierra didn't realize she was still standing in the doorway with her hand tightly wrapped around the straps of her suitcase.

"Well, come on in, Tierra!" Michelle had finally looked away from the laptop. "Did you not have happy time with Gran-Gran?"

"Understatement."

Tierra flopped on her bed, eyes locked on the ceiling. She recalled her father's face when he'd read the Bible to her. Most of the passages he read she couldn't understand, but she liked the smile he gave when he shared its words with her. The memory compelled her to sit up. She looked around the room. The Bible once hidden in her trunk now rested on the desk next to her reading lamp. Since she'd been at school she'd only read about half of a chapter in Genesis. She stared at it, contemplating another attempt at reading it. *Someone really should've given the writers of that thing some constructive criticism.*

"Michelle, are you doing something important over there?"

"For you, I'm never busy." Michelle scoffed then tucked her laptop away. "What's up? What ya need? A shrink? Should I put my shrink cap on? Let me go find it."

Tierra grinned. "Thanks, but do you have anything to drink? Like a real drink?"

Michelle's eyes widened. She smirked as she made her way to the miniature fridge. "Girl, please. Of course I do!" She busied with pouring a homemade concoction that she kept in a lemonade pitcher. Within seconds of handing the foam cup to Tierra, the entire cup's contents had been consumed and Tierra was awaiting another dose.

"That bad, huh?" In answer to Tierra's nod, Michelle took heed and refilled Tierra's cup.

Expecting Tierra to go for a third, she hurried to prepare herself one as well. "No fun drinking alone."

"I think I'll go with you to Lucy's tonight. Maybe take Mr. Cherry up on his offer." Tierra downed her third cup. On its completion she began rummaging through her dresser drawers.

Michelle laughed. "Look at you about to be a cliché."

"I'm not a cliché. I'm not doing this because I have daddy issues or because my grandmother pissed me to the heavens."

"Michelle bit the rim of her cup. "Who said anything about your daddy? Heck I love my daddy. I was actually just poking fun at your apparent rebellion against whatever system you were reminded of when you went home. Either way I'm for bucking the system so you won't get protest here." She emptied the pitcher into her mouth. "We'll have to pick up a bottle on the way. Doggone Cherry is considering having us start paying for our drinks and I'm not trying to give him more of my dollars."

Tierra produced a silk pink short set from her pajama drawer. She held it up to the light. "This might do."

Michelle snatched them from her. "Girl, no. You're not starring in 70's porn. It's a damn club. You need something with a line up your ass."

Tierra tried muffling her laugh. Michelle was waiting for an answer and all she could picture was drawing an actual line up the crack of her butt. Failing the fight, she grinned. Michelle shook her head. "I'm sorry, Michelle. That's what I got, though. Don't tell me I don't qualify for the job now cause that would make me really sad." The giggles were taking over.

"You sure you're ready to do this? Cause if you're going to snicker and snort all night, Cherry is going to walk your ass up out of there."

Tierra finally regained control. "I wasn't before, but I am now. It makes sense to do it. I need to make my own money, pay my own way. Folks think that just because they paid your way they can tell you what to do, how to feel. I can't live like that."

"Okay and what about Caden?"

The recollection of his cologne sent chills up Tierra's spine. She inhaled as though she could smell him in the room. "What about him?"

"Well obviously you're crushing on him. I do have to warn you that he doesn't date girls that work at the club. I know it's a stupid rule, but if you're going to dance there, I think you should know."

Tierra contemplated her attraction to Caden. He seemed like he liked her, but he never actually said that he did. She enjoyed spending time with him, but this was her independence she was weighing against liking a boy. Pieces of her argument with her grandmother began swirling.

When you're an adult having to pay off loans, you'll sing a different tune. You think I would've opted to send you off to school incurring debt if I had the choice not to? It's expensive maintaining my home and your mother's. Whatever money your father left, has gone to doctor's bills, both the ones he left behind and for when Cherish goes through her…whatever it is she goes through.

She could hear her own voice shouting in reply. *Make her get her ass up and get a job! She's ducking life and we all have to pay for it. Why are we letting her do this to us? Now we have to sell ourselves to this Jackson Trent guy just so I can go to school? I'll drop out if that's the case.*

The picture of Madeline, faster than Tierra could've estimated she'd move, reaching for Tierra's face, taking hold of her chin made Tierra's head throb. *This is the second time I've had to check your tongue. If I have to do it again, you won't have one. Don't look away. Now I know you're struggling with the idea of Brandon not being your father. We all are. I imagine so is Jackson. No matter what, Brandon will always be the father that raised you. However, if this man, Jackson, is truly your biological father and your mother and water-walking father never informed him, then you my dear, nor I for that matter, sit high enough to judge or punish him for trying to find some way to connect to you.*

Michelle's finger snaps brought Tierra back to the present. She took a deep breath and held Michelle by the shoulders. "I know it looked like he was that answer to everything I complained about. And I know you take some sort of pride in being the one who introduced me to him, but honestly, Caden is just a boy. Maybe he likes me and maybe he won't. You said it yourself; I could meet a thousand guys if I got out more. Well, what's more out then dancing at Lucy's?"

Michelle shrugged. "This is true. All that logic, that's why you make the straight A's. I for one won't convince you to chase after someone who can't work the nerve to tell you he's feeling you. Who knows what other nerves need working." She giggled. "I'll call Caden to pick us up. Meanwhile, you can come help me with this paper. It's extra credit for Mr. Leonard's class. Apparently, his grading scale isn't a fan of sleeping students. Can't blunder my perfect B record." She clasped her hands and bowed her head. "Please oh brilliant, Tierra. Actually, I should tell him you oversaw my writing. He'd probably pass me without reading."

Tierra agreed to assist. However, what she really wanted was for Michelle to refill the pitcher.

11 LOSING MISS PROPER

Upon arriving at Lucy's, the dressing room was packed. Mr. Cherry bustled through the double doors. Tierra watched as he surveyed the women whilst checking his schedule. Assessing who might be ready to go on next, he barked, "Stick to the schedule, ladies. Why is it so hard to get a damn g-string ready?"

Mr. Cherry flashed his gold tooth smile at the sight of Tierra. *Look it here, my lottery ticket has come back. Didn't realize she was so tall. Hmmm, Princess Tierra has a nice ring to it.* He scratched his palm.

"Good to see you, Miss Tierra!" He kissed her hand. Some of the women chuckled at the over-display of affection. With one glaring eye Mr. Cherry silenced them.

Nerves dancing around Tierra's belly, she blurted, "I need a drink. Do you mind if I run to the bar and order one?" It was then that she recalled she didn't have any pocket money. *Oh crap what if I have to pay for it?*

"I kind of do mind." Mr. Cherry shooed off Michelle then walked Tierra through the dressing room. First thing you need to learn is you don't need to be going out into the crowd like the common folks, unless you're lap dancing. You need to seem close enough to get to, but somewhat out of reach. That's the enticement. I will have Corinne bring you a taste for now. What's your vice?"

Tierra had no knowledge of alcohol. She only knew that she liked the concoctions that Michelle mixed back at the dorms. She glanced over at Michelle. *Maybe this is a mistake. I don't even know what I like.*

Michelle darted over and whispered in Tierra's ear, "Vodka and pineapple tonic. Stick with what we were already drinking. You don't want to mix liquors and be throwing up all over stage." Thankful, Tierra nodded.

Mr. Cherry smirked. "Don't tell me you already have a Manager. Will you be conferring with Michelle on your song selections as well? Maybe your underwear choices too?" He snickered.

Tierra grinned. "Don't mind Michelle. I'll just have a vodka and pineapple tonic."

Mr. Cherry nodded. He eyed Michelle then gave the waitress, Corinne the go ahead. "Miss Michelle, don't be on your mess tonight."

Michelle forced a grin. Once he turned his head, she slipped a white pill under her tongue. Catching Tierra's glimpse, she shook her head, mouthing the lack of need to worry.

Mr. Cherry pulled Tierra aside. "In the meantime, you can get dressed. I know you're new to this so it's okay to let the other girls guide you through, maybe not Michelle though. She's a bit of a loose cannon at times, clumsy. I've allowed you to waste my time and hang around distracting Caden the past few times you've been in, but don't take my kindness lightly. If you're here to work, you're welcome. If not, you need to sit in the audience and pay for a dance like anyone else. Hold a sec." He jogged behind a six foot amazon heading for the back door. "Noodle! Please get your beautiful afro crowned self out there. You're up next. I'll have Tierra come on after you."

On cue the waitress had made it back with Tierra's order. She rushed the liquid down her throat, holding her breath until the end.

Corinne smiled. "This other one is yours too. Figured you might need a little extra." Tierra grabbed the second glass and repeated her guzzle. "Thanks"

The waitress nodded and slid an aluminum ball into her hand. "In case of an emergency."

Confused, Tierra accepted the offer. The woman proceeded to serve Michelle. Tierra pocketed the ball then ducked into the bathroom.

She leaned over the corner sink and inspected her face. "Okay, Miss Tierra, breathe. You can do this. It'll be fun, right? First time for everything. And it's not even really your first time. You saw how they reacted last time. Just a slightly larger crowd, that's all."

Mr. Cherry spotted Tierra as she emerged from the bathroom. She was dressed in a pink and white, striped button-down and black pump. He stared as he tipped Corinne. Although Mr. Cherry was eager for the crowd to see Tierra dance, he had a standard to uphold. His girls always performed in the most exposing, exotic pieces of string; seductive straps of lace, even accessories were chosen with a purpose. Not one of them would ever go out on stage without being fully prepared to put on a professional show. A few may have gone on with more liquor in their bosoms than he would like, but they were all fierce when they got up on that stage. *It's obvious the child is a rookie. I should've required her to train. But she's so damn sexy in that inexperienced way. It's been a long time since we've had a girl who wasn't jaded yet.* He sighed.

Recognizing the budding fury on Mr. Cherry's face, one of the pot smoker veterans spoke up for Tierra. "Let her dance, Cherry. We need some new blood out there. She'd got that whole slept over her man's house look. Trust me, as long as she's taking them clothes off, the tricks out there wouldn't care if she had on a winter coat."

Tierra pointed her chin. It was an effort to avoid her now light head from drifting away. Sweat began to trickle down the back of her legs. Mr. Cherry's face was becoming blurry. She built herself up as sassy and confident. Now here she was looking like she was having a high school sleepover. *I'm blowing it. And my head is going to blow away like a balloon and then how will I go get it back?* She pictured herself running, headless chasing the string of her detached head.

"You know what, go ahead. But I promise you if I lose any business behind you and your untrained ass, you'll never step foot in here again. I don't care how you do tonight, tomorrow you're coming in and learning that stage."

The DJ welcomed, "Princess Tierra." Not knowing if she should pose, Tierra was still. A shiver travelled up her spine. *Please Lord, I know this isn't your thing, but could you please not show the whole place I'm terrified?*

The music began its thump. Tierra wasn't sure what to do. Her insides warmed. She closed her eyes. Decidedly, she swung her hips. A woman in the crowd yelled out, "All right baby, I ain't got all night! Get low or do something!" The crowd roared in agreement.

Tierra focused on the fire that was building in her limbs. Eventually the only sounds she could hear was the crooner's defiance, *All I need is a beautiful girl so me and her can fuck the world.* Swerving her shoulders, then circling her waist, her temperature was rising. The first two buttons of her shirt became undone. Beads of sweat glistened off of her skin.

From the foot of the stage, Tierra heard, "That's right baby, get in your groove. I don't mind a little slow ramp up. Let me see you from the back. I like that back!"

Tierra made it her mission to gratify. She touched her toes. An increasing number of spectators drew near. Grinding against one of the center poles, she could feel the dollars being tossed as they collided with her legs. First there were two, followed behind three quick breezes of paper flying toward her. Suddenly there was paper falling all around her. Tierra smiled, wondering if any of the bills were larger than ones. The money accumulated beneath her feet. For fear of slipping, she opened her eyes.

"Girl, I ought to take you off that stage and eat you up right here."

Her voice is higher than a mountain and she got the nerve to look like a dude on work release? Does she realize how high pitch her voice is? The woman, dressed in a Carhartt jacket and timberland boots licked her lips. To Tierra's surprise, she noticed there was another woman beside her. Her charcoal suit was tailor fit and the diamonds in her ears weren't overstated, although easy to recognize. She didn't yell out commands like the other woman. She simply nodded like she was giving Tierra the parental "okay" to continue. *Who knew I'd be the women's flavor?*

"I see you looking at me baby, just keep dancing. I got enough twenty-dollar bills here to pay your rent," shouted a man competing for Tierra's attention. He squeezed between the two women like an enthusiastic fan attending a pop concert.

Tierra's skin glistened under the fluorescent lights. She rocked back and forth, gliding her fingers up her thighs. Each button she unlatched gave the crowd a resurgence of energy. Wrapping her legs around the pole inspired a shower of dollar bills. Her zest urging her to grind into a split, she surprised herself with her own flexibility. Seductively, she arose, loosening the last of her buttons. Finally removing her blouse, she tossed it into the audience. There wasn't a soul in the house that wasn't on fire and totally engrossed in, Princess Tierra.

By the end of the tune, Tierra had bills pouring from her underwear. More carpeted the stage. There were shouts, howls, and random voices, begging for encores and screaming phone number requests. Grinning and waving, Tierra scooped her earnings from the stage. As she backed into the dressing room, a waitress came over with a bucket. "After you dump in your bag or wherever, return the bucket to the bar."

Gleefully, Tierra agreed, stuffing what she saw to be twenty and fifty-dollar bills into the pail. Once she returned to the dressing room, she found her book bag and transferred the money inside. *I should count it. But I can't count in front of everyone, isn't that tacky? How will I know if someone steals any though?* She looked around the room then remembered she saw lockers near the bathroom. Scurrying over to see there were any free, she found one on the bottom row with an opened lock. She placed her bag inside, stuffing the key between her breasts.

Still fueled from her stage performance, Tierra searched for Michelle. Finding her blowing smoke through her nostrils near the back door of the dressing room, Tierra was disappointed. "So you didn't see me do my thing?"

Michelle chuckled. "Girl, yes. I watched for a second. Once I saw you pop those buttons I knew you were good. Let me find out you got some freak in you." She passed Tierra the joint she was smoking.

Tierra sucked in the smoke. Inhaling enough smoke to send a S.O.S, Tierra coughed. Her chest caved.

Michelle patted her back. "Honey I forget you new to it all. My fault."

Tierra's coughing subsided. She could feel her cheeks radiating. "Sorry. Maybe smoking isn't for me."

Michelle shrugged. "Maybe. But here try another pull. This time, make it short like you're breathing it in but a regular breath, not like a yoga breath."

Tierra tried again. The smoke gently floated through her lungs. Blowing it back into the atmosphere felt like she was blowing bricks off of her shoulders. "Michelle, do you think I have to dance on the laps of the men *and* the women out there?" She took another drag of Michelle's joint before handing it back.

"Not if you don't want to. Most of the girls do it to make some extra money. I do it sometimes. They certainly tip better."

Corinne was back for her rounds. She brought recovery drinks for each of the dancers already done with their sets. With some, she exchanged what looked like pieces of paper that she pulled from her apron. The dancers would hand her a few dollars from their pot. Business-like, she announced to the room, "Ladies, they tipping like crazy out there. Tierra, you the bomb cause you got them all in their feelings. A couple patrons asked about private shows. Mr. Cherry ought to be ecstatic."

Blushing, Tierra reconciled her indecisiveness. *Hmm. Aren't private shows where they sometimes have sex? That'll be a no for me. But I could bless them with a few lap dances. Heck, I could probably make enough to pay my tuition within a week.*

Corrine added, "Look if you're going to do it, chill on them drinks. Dab some more perfume on your wrists cause you can't go out smelling like smoke. You should take your time and only dance for the ones spending money on drinks. At least it's their liquor they smell."

Michelle chimed in, "Sometimes they get so drunk, they just give you everything they have in their pockets. One guy gave me his actual wallet." She laughed then pressed the nail bit of joint remaining against the wall. "Just have fun. We'll have loads to talk about in the morning."

Tierra retreated to her locker. There she found the ball of aluminum Corinne handed her previously. She found that it held two white tablets. Curious but unsure how drastic the effects could be, she bit one pill in half then re-enclosed the remainder.

Out on the floor, every color in the room seeming brighter than before and Tierra's limbs were yearning to move. With each dance, Tierra opened her legs a little wider, swirled her hips with more intent, and straddled with audacity. She offered her behind to faces and fondled her own breasts. *Damn, I wish Caden were vying for a dance. I feel amazing.*

The executive woman waved her dollars. Tierra strutted over and wrapped her legs around her. She stuffed three fifty-dollar bills in Tierra's brassiere. Tierra shook her breasts then leaned in close enough for the woman to smell them. Enticed by Tierra's performance, the woman whispered, "How much to let me taste you?"

Tierra stood and bent over. She bounced as the woman flapped a stack of money on her behind. Slipping her own finger in her underwear, taking a swipe at the wet, Tierra then turned to the woman. "How much money you got?"

12 CHERISH THE LOVE

Storm clouds hovered over the streets. Gushes of rain slapped plants into aggressive sways, as the wind seemed to be scooping raindrops, then emptying them in buckets. Balancing an umbrella over head with one hand, Madeline jiggled her key in the lock of her daughter's home with the other. She flurried through the door with a quick turnaround, pulling the umbrella to a close, but then reopened the umbrella inside and rested it on the floor alongside the base of the coat tree. Her trench coat soaked, she hung like a used handkerchief on the wooden stems.

"Geez, it's really coming down out there. It's a good thing I planned to stay over tonight." She tugged at her scarf until it loosened.

Putting the last of the dried dishes away in an upper cabinet, Marcia, the housekeeper, lent a delicate grin. "Don't you smile at me like that,

Marcia. Cherish can hear me. She's in her zone again today, but not brain dead, although I'm sure she'd like me to believe that." Marcia nodded. "I didn't mean anything by it, Ms. Madeline. She actually wished me a good afternoon when I got here today. We had a pleasant exchange until that Mr. Trent started calling."

In the living area, the television was on the Jazz Music Channel. Cherish sat still in what used to be Brandon's armchair as she stared at the digital photo flashes of musicians. Disinterested in the facts bannered across the screen, Cherish stared off into a distance that was unreachable by anyone or anything searching for a connection.

Madeline seated herself at the edge of the couch. Next to her was the end table, which held an 8x10 black and white framed photo of Cherish holding Tierra as a newborn. Tierra, swaddled in the standard striped hospital cloth, was in an angelic sleep. Cherish, dressed in a long, black maxi dress showed no physical signs of a recent delivery. Her smile was like she had been presented with a lottery prize check. Her image was captured, posing Tierra in front of the mirror that hung on the wall near the front door.

As many times as Madeline studied the photo, today was the first time she noticed the reflection of Brandon's prideful glare behind the camera. It was only a glimpse, as he must've been trying his best to stay out of the photo. Madeline held the frame. "Whatever you were hiding, Cherish, I know you couldn't hide it from Brandon. Jackson told me Brandon reached out to him. You can't keep mum about this forever. Your past has found you. I suspect it's a song everyone has to one day sing." Madeline sighed.

Cherish had her own battle of emotions whenever she viewed the snapshot. It was why she would sometimes visit the family room in the wee hours of the night. She faced it every time she sat in Brandon's chair. Each time with tears on her heart she recollected Brandon's loyalty, his love, and his idealistic ownership of what he understood to be, "unconditional."

****
****

"Brandon, we have to talk." A teenage Cherish closed the door to her mother's house behind her. She wanted to get out everything she had rehearsed to say while they were still on the porch. It was more for Brandon than it was for her. With certainty she knew that what she was about to confess would break his heart. He was a sensitive man. It wasn't a hard conclusion to get to when she witnessed his despair after a football game where his team almost lost by three points. He blamed every aspect of the near fail on himself. For the rest of the week he'd come over after practice and lay his head in her lap while she rubbed his head. They'd sit in silence, pretending to be interested in the news reports of house fires and ribbon cuttings on the television, both wanting to talk about the game, but she never knew how to confront the imagination of something lost.

"Baby, I just got here. Why are you looking so serious already? I couldn't have done anything wrong, yet. Could I?" Nerves running amuck in the pit of his stomach, Brandon chuckled dryly. When Cherish failed to return even so much as a smile, he imagined that she was going to tell him that being together was too much for her. Being the girlfriend of a fickle athlete was taking a toll on her mental and emotional health and she could no longer be his wife-to-be. Given what looked to be her greening cheeks, he was relieved to consider that maybe it wasn't a break-up, but Cherish was sick and dying. But then the thought of her dying panicked him again; if that was her news then he'd better take this moment seriously. His eyes burned as he pictured standing at her grave, lowering her into the ground. He quickly brushed away the tears, deciding that he needed to be strong for her. Whatever it was, he had to love her enough to allow her to tell it without the pressure of his emotions. "Cherish, what's wrong? Whatever it is, you can tell me."

****

****

Marcia handed both Madeline and Cherish a child-sized cup of applesauce, each with a plastic spoon. Mechanically, Cherish accepted her cup. After thanking Marcia, Madeline peeled hers open and returned her attention to Cherish. With the first spoonful, she updated Cherish on Tierra's progress.

"You'd be so proud of Tierra. She called yesterday and said she got an, 'A' on her English midterm paper. Tell you the truth, I was relieved he wasn't still fuming. The way she stormed out of the house when I told her about Jackson. Just so many twists to our stories, you know?" She sighed. "Oh anyway, she wrote about Brandon, a good memory. When he would take her to the amusement parks and buy her cotton candy. She still remembers those summers. It was sweet really. I'll have to have her read it to you. She has this roommate, Michelle, whom she seems to adore. You know Tierra never had too many friends growing up. That's your trait right there, blocking everyone out. Remember your one girlfriend, Lanaeya? I liked her. Anyhow, it's good to know she made a connection with someone. I tell you, God is good! When Tierra calls she sounds so happy. It reminds me of when Brandon would call while he was away at school, particularly when he first left, you'd get so excited. You wouldn't know what to do with yourself. When you two would finish speaking, you'd fervently tell me what had to be every detail of your conversation. Back then, Brandon was your

best friend, but I knew I was a close second."
Madeline's voice trailed off.

****
****

"I'm pregnant. I swear I didn't know
when we agreed to get married. I swear."

Silence. Brandon had a way of biting his
bottom lip when he was trying to find the right
words. *Boy, he's really tearing into that lip. This has got
to be the worst day of my life. I should just abort it. Why
didn't I abort it? He didn't have to know. How could I do
this to him?*

****
****

Madeline knew her child missed Brandon
and she hoped, Tierra. When the three of them
were a family, Cherish seemed content, hopeful

for Tierra's future. Now Tierra was away at college and the girl would only seldom hear her mother tell her how proud of her she was. Madeline stroked Cherishes face. "Oh Cherish, I just wish you'd talk to me. Talk to Tierra even. She's got a ton of questions. And she's angry. Despite all that cheer she tried to muster up on the phone, I know she is. Who wouldn't be? Confused, scared, and just like you she's shutting down. I wish I knew what was going on in that pretty little head of yours."

****
****

"It's his."

Just the sound of Brandon's acknowledgement of Trent churned Cherish's stomach. "Maybe not, Brandon; I don't know that for sure. I only found out last week. Haven't been to the doctor yet." She shuffled her feet. *Stupid liar. Why'd you have to tell him that? It sounds so stupid. You sound stupid. Who breaks this news without going to the doctor first? Way to go Cherish. Just keep hurting him. This is such a nightmare. He'll never marry you now. I just wish everything could go back to the beginning. This is so horrible. It just ruins everything. I'm going to abort it. I should tell him that. I can't have this baby. What am I thinking? What if it's really Jackson's? I can't have Jackson's baby. How could I even consider it? I'm so disgusting. How will I face my mother? Brandon's father?*

"I'm sterile."

"What? Brandon, how do you know that? Why do you know that? How can you be sterile? That can't be true."

"My mom. She had an "episode" during one of her visits. My father thinks I don't remember, but I do. I was five at the time. She accused me of being my father's spy. Said I was watching her for him. She complained that I was the one locking all the doors in the house. I was the reason why she couldn't get any air. She wanted to break free. In her mind, I was stopping her. My father used to try to let her watch me when he was at work, you know, as a peace offering after he got full custody. And probably to force my grandmother to think that my mother wasn't a total screw up. One day after my father left for work, she packed her bags with everything she thought was valuable that we had in the house. I came into the bedroom and asked where she was going. She yelled something about a clever plot to kill her then pushed me. I fell. Her eyes went dark. I don't think she knew who I was at that point. She kicked and kicked until she saw my blood. Maybe then she realized what she did, I don't know. She cried, apologized, and then ran out of the house. I never saw her again. Doctor said I could never have children. I was going to tell you before we got married. I had been working up the nerve, but I see you were working with your own nerves."

Cherish's veins sizzled. Her bladder was filling. She never fathomed Brandon had suffered such a tragedy. She wanted to hold him. Dry the tears he had yet to cry. But who was she to comfort him? It was she who was his torturer this time. When she pictured the true father of her child, her throat swelled with salt pebbles, sucking the moisture right out of her gums. The morning's eggs were pooling in her chest. Rising. "Excuse me." She darted inside to the bathroom where she hurled the contents of her stomach over the toilet. Facing her bile, she wished she could flush her head down the drain along with it. *He must really hate me. And then to leave him standing there after he just told me something so painful. He must think I'm the worst person ever. Maybe I am.*

"Are you okay?" Cherish hadn't noticed that Brandon followed her into the house. He let her have her privacy, but once he was certain she was done, he spoke up.

"I'm sorry, Brandon."

"Don't be. I love you more than anything. We can't let this destroy us unless you'd prefer to be with him."

Vigorously, she shook her head. "No, no, no. I prefer you, I swear."

"Well then I'm going to marry you and be that child's father. That is if you will accept me as such."

Cherish was speechless. She searched his face to find the clue that this man was not a man at all but an angel sent directly from the heavens. He interrupted her search by pulling her closer to him. His arms wrapped tightly around her shoulders, he brought her head to his chest. She could hear the steady beating of his heart. It was as if the shame and pain were commanded to keep at bay. She was with her protector now. That's when she knew they'd be alright. As long as he continued to hold her she could face the world and forget Jackson.

****
****

Madeline studied Cherishes face for any sign of interaction. Cherish turned to her and smiled. It was a soft shy smile. The kind Cherish would give when she was being complimented. A smile that said, *Thank you. You're kinder than I deserve.* But Madeline knew it wasn't truly directed at her. She seemed to be looking past her. It was as if someone was standing at Madeline's shoulder and that was whom Cherish was giving her gratitude and hope to.

13 THE PLACES WE GO

Lucy's was standing room only. Smoke filled the great room. Mr. Cherry was quite proud of his ceiling held fog machines. He came from an error where smoking was acceptable in public places. *Damn new age government trying to kill the sexiness in the business. Who the hell thought taxing the sex industry was a good idea? Probably someone's son who couldn't get laid or paid. Ha!* Often he repeated the joke to himself. Each time he'd laugh like someone else was telling it to him and it was the funniest thing he'd heard in ages.

A party of eight shouted and hooted like they were promoting a drinking contest at a college fraternity party. Tierra watched, as they bought round after round of drinks. *That's the only table I'll need for the night. That's for sure.*

After just three weeks of working only two nights a week, Tierra had settled into a routine with the other girls. Dressed in a sheer black teddy and a yellow satin garter belt, her oiled curves fit in like she was working with lifetime intentions. She strutted passed the customer restrooms and into the dressing room.

Peggy, one of meatier women working at Lucy's, bounced in. Her golden skin was flawless like she had never lost the sweet round softness afforded to her as a baby. Blue contacts and a blonde wig confused those curious about her race. She liked it that way. *Let them flip them dollars while they asking them stupid ass questions.* Tierra found her peculiar. At the end of each night she'd catch the ear of one of the girls and go off on a tangent about how over-concerned people were about race and complexions. Then she'd spew facts and figures relating to her opinions of welfare and the government. Once she got going, she'd talk over anyone with anything to add. Much of the time the girls would dress and simply nod. As if invited to continue her soapbox rants, she'd accompany them on the way out to their cars.

"Gotta love those University men, right Tierra? They come in ready to spend. I swear the pole tricks and titty rubs have been brewing in their imaginations before you flicker a butt cheek."

Tierra nodded although unsure where Peggy was aiming at. Still, the revelation that the college crew would be generous was what she wanted to hear. In less than an hour she could probably be done for the night. She could catch a cab and get back to the dorm to soak her feet. *Why is it that only when I'm fully dressed in here I remember how much I hate high heels?*

"I forgot you're a Newbie. You haven't had the sweet feeling of annoying ass college boys spending their parent's money on your beautiful self. Girl, go out there before they're all tapped out. Or worst, somebody's mom comes to collect them. That's happened before, you know." Peggy held up a wad of folded dollars. "I ain't selfish. Besides, you need to build that tough skin if you're going to work here. Them drunk behinds will call you every derogatory name in the book like they hate you, but then give you all of their money. Sick freaks!"

Tierra smiled, trying her best to appear grateful for the advice. Peggy turned her attention to the mirror. Tierra let out the breath she had been trapping. *Boys my age never fooled with me too much. They always glance over then go for Michelle. Maybe if I smell like a touch of weed, they'll think I'm cool. Heck I'll probably need some to endure all the hooting and hollering Peggy said they do anyway. Like why do you need to yell from across the table? I get it. You're turned on. I'm here to serve. We all know our roles.*

Over by the restroom, there were the usual smokers seated on the floor. They sat across from one of the mirrors, admiring the different shapes they were able to make by blowing smoke. Once, the last smoker alerted the others the joint was finished, the cluster of women all squeezed together to see the details of their reflections.

They each dabbled at fixing hair or make up. Tierra chuckled. *They look like they're trying to fit in a photo booth. You'd think they didn't know we had a whole wall of mirrors in here.*

"So, I know I don't really know you all that well, but can I buy some of that smoke off of you? It's like five dollars, right?"

The women laughed. "Girl, you're not even a smoker."

"You ain't fitting to waste up my weed."

"Excuse me? I just asked to buy some, not for an analysis on what I'll do with it."

The woman who caught her eye in the mirror turned to her. "You're not a smoker. Now, I know this because if you were, you'd know that ain't nobody trying to waste up a bag of good smoke on you choking up a lung. Don't matter how much you pay, and it won't be five dollars by the way. Mr. Cherry ain't coming in here with his head on fire cause we got the new girl drinking up all his good liquor cause her damn chest on fire."

Tierra was taken aback but decided to play it cool. There was a table full of paying customers she needed to get to. "No, I'm not a smoker. You're right. But I can't find Corinne."

Another woman Tierra dubbed the leader of the crew, grinned. While the others gave her pursed lips and crooked necks, this woman in her leather and zippers ensemble watched while she touched up her foundation. Sensing Tierra was about to accept the rejection, she turned to face her.

"So, you want to get high? I get it. Lots of girls need it to do what we do. But you're not about to pass out on my watch or dollar. Cause we smoke that real. None of the bull from the corner guys." She handed Tierra a re-rolled cigar from her clutch. "Here, take a hit. Two pulls that's it. You'll be as high as you need to be. If you feel like you can handle it then maybe some other night I'll sell you a bag. Not tonight though.

Corinne's around and she'd prefer to get you what you're used to. I ain't stepping on those toes."

Afraid the woman would rescind the offer; Tierra grabbed quickly took the blunt and held it to her lips. Coached by the woman's nodding, Tierra inhaled gradually. There was a sea of clouds gathering in her head. The room seemed quiet despite everyone's bustling. The girls coached her not to rush the second hit. She inhaled slowly, taking the smoke into her chest.

Tierra appreciated the airiness under her limbs. All tension had miraculously withered away. She made a mental note to smoke with these women before the next time she went on stage. *Corinne better stop playing or I'm going to start getting my stuff from them. I could've killed it if I felt like this earlier!*

As Tierra was coming from the back, Noodle was taking the last of her tips from the unruly group of college men. Tierra's breathing became heavy and her palms dampened. *Calm down. We can all get money here tonight. Isn't that what Peggy said? Noodle has been doing this a minute. She's got to make her money too. No one is going to save tables for you.*

Tierra focused on the rowdy table of patrons and began her strut. As the faces became clearer, she realized they weren't as young as she initially thought. The attractive goateed ring-leader waving a double-stacked wad of dollars was of particular interest. *Mr. Leonard?* Instantly, the rapturous fog that floated her head a moment before, escaped only to be trapped in her belly.

Corinne spotted Tierra. She noticed the girl had stopped moving. Corinne glanced over at Mr. Cherry who was standing by the bar, keeping watch on the crowd near the stage. She hurried over to Tierra. "Everyone gets that look the first time they see someone they know. You know him right?"

"Sort of. You think if I act like there's a problem, Caden or somebody will throw him out?"

"Not the route you want to take, trust me." Corinne scoffed, "You're trippin' anyway. He's spending too much money. I could give you this double shot of Hennessey, right here though. Drink it quick before Mr. Cherry sees you. Once it hits your head you should get over all that pesky shy business. Besides, if he's half as embarrassed as you are, he'll spend that whole stack out of guilt. Seen it too many times."

"Isn't this someone else's drink? You don't have anything else?"

"I'll get them another one. You got too much conversation for something so simple. Let me tell you something, this is just the first time. You're going to run into all types of familiar faces in here. I know what you want, that pill. But you ain't offering up no paper for it, so, take my kind little drink offer and go handle your business!"

Tierra was determined to defeat the nervous tingles that numbed her knees and gurgled her belly. She snatched the shot glass, taking in every drop of the liquid at once. Without asking, she went for the other glass on the tray and gulped its contents too.

Corinne was unfazed. "You're so dramatic. Like I said, nothing new."

Tierra returned to the dressing room. She dabbed her wrists and inner thighs with a fruit inspired body oil. She didn't want any trouble for reeking of liquor.

Michelle hurried in and announced that Mr. Cherry was starting the second show. The first three girls who went on had to stay backstage so the rest could go work the crowd. Michelle was going back out to work the floor.

Tierra headed back out into the awaiting audience. She wondered if Michelle had also spotted Mr. Leonard. *She couldn't have. She'd be teasing me if she did. Or at least be just as freaked out, no?*

Mr. Cherry routed his way over to her. "Hey Princess. You're on after Noodle. So you need to get in the back."

Tierra's jitters returned. "You think I could get a shot of Hennessy? I promise I won't take more than a shot."

"Oh no, honey. I've been watching you and you've had more than enough. We can't have you losing the contents of your stomach all over the crowd, now can we? Plus it smells like you might've been fraternizing with the potheads."

"Saw someone she knows," Corinne blurted as she walked by. She ignored Tierra's glare. Continuing on to serve Peggy a chocolate martini, she added, "I got something for her if you want, but she can't keep getting freebies."

Before Tierra could narrow her eyes, Mr. Cherry responded. "Don't tell me you got her on that shit too. Well, it's better than her smelling like a damn back alley."

Scurrying to her locker, Tierra grinned. Corinne followed for payment. "I thought you was trying to throw me under the bus, but thanks. Had I known Mr. Cherry wouldn't mind me taking those pills you got, I would have been said something."

Corinne nodded. "You ain't got to keep doing all that talking." When Tierra handed her a twenty-dollar bill, Corinne dipped her hand into her apron. She produced a sandwich bag with three tablets in it. "Since I only got three left, you can get them all for twenty. I'm not feeding you anymore, though. Your mama and them must've spoiled you. The way you just expect is crazy. Seem like everyone battery packing it. Not me, though."

Back on the club floor, Tierra happened across Michelle, whose legs were wrapped around a man resembling someone's grandfather. Her back was arched, head leaned, and hips gyrating.

Tierra shouted over the music. "You mind if I borrow your glasses from your locker?"

Michelle nodded her approval, careful not to break her concentration. A bald gentleman with whiskers of a mustache from the adjoining table grabbed Tierra by the arm. "Won't you stay a moment?" He laid a few dollars next to his glass. Tierra mustered a smile. "After my set."

Back in the dressing room Tierra swallowed one of the pills she scored from Corinne. She thought about the wad of cash stuffed into her book bag. *Mr. Leonard can't judge me. If anything, I can judge him for being here. He's been smiling in my face since the beginning of the semester. I'm going to go out there and show him what he and I both know he's been craving.*

Meeka, a performer dressed in a white corset with black ribbons and matching g-string, burst through the dressing room doors. Taking note of the two pills left in the baggie Tierra was holding, she asked, "Let me get one? That wack weed with all them seeds that Carmen had has a high that lasts all of twenty minutes. And for the way they got that money flowing out there..." She shook her head. "Anyhow, you want to sell me one? Corinne on the other side of the floor."

As Tierra was still contemplating Meeka's offer, Meeka counted out fifty dollars and stuffed it into her hand. She helped herself to the bag and removed a pill. "I know I overpaid, but I gotta get out there. You just came up." She chuckled then swallowed the pill whole.

By the time Tierra's name was announced, she felt like she had been floating. She took inventory of how sexy her fellow dancers were with their rounded posteriors and deliberate sways. She felt her own provocative impulses intensifying. Equipped with Michelle's oversized sunglasses, her cubic zirconia studs glistened under the stage lights. The black stilettos, formally

known as her *church shoes*, gave added oomph to
her calves, complimenting the thickness of her
thighs. She casually strolled to the center of the
stage like she was about to present an opening
monologue. The crowd cheered.

Caden stood in the back of the room near
the emergency exit. He attentively watched as
Tierra humped the first of three silver poles.
Tierra's mysteriously muddled sensitivity was
what he found most attractive about her. Sure,
she was occasionally a know-it-all, but there was
some innocence her smart remarks couldn't hide.
When he met her he hadn't pegged her as the
free-spirited exhibitionist he was looking at. Her
facial features were soft, free of the creases and
lines that became hardened by life's
disappointments. Somehow she was able to
intrigue him with her contradictions. *Miss Tierra, I
just can't nail you down.*

Michael Leonard gawked at the familiar
woman dancing on stage. *Is that Tierra Proper?*

When he accepted his adjunct colleagues'
invitation, he never fathomed that one of his
students would be whom he'd watch disrobe. Still,
he couldn't take his eyes off of her. *Is this even
allowed? What am I talking about? I can't control where
she works. This is my free time. The school can't monitor
where I play. And my God, her body is phenomenal.*

Michael Leonard was entranced. He
zombied over to the stage. Stuffing a hundred-
dollar bill in the side of Tierra's thong, he hoped
to be noticed. She neglected to face him. Still he
stared up at her, his eyes tracing her round places.
She continued to command the stage. Her focus
unbroken; to her, he could have been anyone. He
longed to see closer, for her to see him. As she
slid down the pole, her head to the ground, he
caught her eye. Another hundred he slid between
her breasts.

Since the first day she walked into his
classroom and took her seat by the window, the
sun illuminating her eyes, Michael had been trying

to shake the urge to imagine her naked. Now here she was right in front of him, sliding her panties down to her ankles. While he stood at the foot of the stage with what was now a full congregation of men and women, staring, she suggestively swayed her body in his direction. When she dropped to her knees then began to crawl, out came another three hundred-dollar bills.

Caden kept watch. His eye was on the suspendered gentleman in awe at the front near the stage. He made himself believe it was because he didn't want some drunken customer to mess around and yank Tierra off the stage. *She has no idea how crazy these guys can be. C'mon Tierra, stick to the middle so I don't have to come get this guy.* The instinct to cover her up and tell her she'd never have to dance again if she just let him take care of her was one he pushed down to his shins. *Stop this, man. If you were really able to take care of her would you be working the door?* However, the more she swung her hips, the more her hair swept her bare skin, the more he empathized with the man lurking at the front of the stage. She was hypnotic.

When Tierra's dance number was over, Michael returned to his seat. *She's incredible!* When she danced, everything else in his world stopped moving. Everyone in the club, not just him, held their breath to hold on to the experience of watching her move. Yet, he was certain that no one could appreciated the show the way he did.

Caden was relieved that Tierra's performance was finally over. He could go back to making sure the club was secure and not worrying about some overzealous patron abducting her. It was hard being on point when he too had to force himself to turn away so people wouldn't realize he, at times, was stimulated. He'd had his share of women and learned early in the game not to sleep with the ones who worked at the club. Many of them weren't looking for a relationship, not serious like he was. He'd overhear a conversation about a customer one of the girls pleased for some extra cash and it'd disappoint him. Twice he had to tell women he dated from the club that the relationship wasn't working after he realized they expected him to spend all his money on them like he was just one of the customers. One girl would entice a patron to the point of thinking they were being invited to be intimate. Then she'd expect Caden to swoop in and save her like an overprotective pimp. She'd conjure a similar scheme every night until Mr. Cherry realized what she was doing and fired her.

Something told Caden that Tierra was different. She didn't belong there. So many of the girls went to school and found dancing as an easy way to earn money, which he could appreciate. But those girls got in and got out. They didn't drink and they hardly smoked. They danced, smiled, got money and went home. Michelle did it because her mother hated it. He chuckled. *I love Michelle. Never one to over-complicate things.*

Although Tierra was sensuous, she had something else in her. There was another version of her, one he'd never seen, and hiding beneath the parts he had already met. Maybe that was the magic that made customers drool. Maybe that was the potion that spelled Caden and every other man she encountered. Maybe he wasn't as different from the customers after all and like anyone else, he had a thing for a good girl who acted bad.

Caden searched the crowd and found Tierra in a far off corner. She had a crowd of men around, one being the entranced man from the foot of the stage. Tierra whined her hips and allowed the man to spank her while the other men rained money upon her and yanked on her underwear. She teased with her pelvis only a smidge away from the man's face. Caden had to tell himself to look away.

Over at Mr. Leonard's table, Michael whispered to Tierra, "Miss Tierra, why don't you remove those sunglasses. Let me see your eyes."

Tierra smirked. She bent over and whispered in his ear, "Mr. Leonard, you can see everything you need to, in your office. Maybe on a stack of papers." Sure, she had his full attention, Tierra winked then moved on to another set of customers.

Her cockiness was evident in her stride. Tierra owned the new woman she was becoming, the sexy seductress. For the first time she was in control of her own life. She'd survive without the looming eye of her grandmother, the lies of her mother, or the apologetic funding of Mr. Jackson Trent. The world would no longer throw its fists at her chin. Now, people had no choice but to acknowledge her womanhood. And she was going to give anyone watching one hell of a show.

14 A TRUTH FOR A TRUTH

Cherish climbed the porch stairs of her mother's home. The lined pots offered struggling branches some solid soil. *Goodness, I guess she'll never get in the habit of bringing those pots in before Christmas.* As she reached the screen door, Madeline opened the heavy door to let her in.

"I thought I heard you. You're starting to shuffle your feet like an old woman."

Cherish smiled meekly. She followed her mother inside, choosing to grab two of the flowerpots to accompany her. Careful not to drop them, she balanced them by holding them into the bosom of her wool coat. Meanwhile, the straps of her oversized pocketbook glided down her arm and weighted wrist.

Locking the door behind Cherish, Madeline then took the pots from her. "When you were a girl you complained that I'd leave the pots in the cold like orphaned children. I guess it's still a peeve."

"I just don't understand. You can hang lights on them if you wanted to, but you just leave them out there for the world to see them dying." Cherish took a wooden hanger from the coat closet then stuffed her coat in between the too many coats hanging. "Tierra's at school. I feel like this closet shouldn't be so full."

Walking the frigid flowerpots into the kitchen, Madeline called behind her. "And I feel like you have a lot to say for someone who hasn't had a thing to say for months. Come on in this kitchen and help me empty these pots."

Although Cherish knew it was ill-advised for her not to follow Madeline's command, she hesitated. Her mother's tone suggested there was something she wanted to discuss. No doubt it had to do with Jackson. *I wonder how mad she'll be if I just run out of here.* Seemingly by instinct, her mother called her name.

"I know what you're doing and you better not disappear. Bring yourself in here and don't make me ask again. Between you and Tierra, I swear it's two teenage girls I got to deal with."

Cherish swallowed the hunk of fear that gathered in her throat. Slowly, she joined her mother in the kitchen. The pots were already empty. Judging by the amount of dirt crowding the base of the trashcan, Madeline made haste in dumping the soil. Cherish watched as her mother swept the mess. The woman handed Cherish the dustpan. As silently instructed, Cherish bent to receive the dirt then dump it. She sighed.

"Judging by that sigh, you know what I want to talk about. It's time, Cherish." Madeline collected the empty dustpan and attached it to the broom. She stashed the two away in the corner behind the garbage can. "It's time for a lot of things. There's something I need to tell you as well. I figure if I'm going to ask you to tell me your secret thoughts, I need to tell you mine."

Her voice was strained. Up all night crying had taken its toll. It pained her to share what she had kept from everyone, but she was convinced that it was her secrets that begat Cherish's.

The shaking in her mother's voice frightened Cherish. *Is she sick? No Mommy, please don't tell me I'm going to lose you too. I've been so selfish in hiding my affair. I'd tell you all my secrets if the Lord would let me keep you.* "I'm sorry," Cherish panicked out. "My silence was, is selfish. I'm sorry. You're the most important person in my life. If this is about your health, I will be there just as you've been for me."

Madeline nodded then pulled a chair from the table. "Let's sit." She patted the table as she typically did when she wanted someone to join her. The fear in Cherish's eyes was unmistakable. If only she had news of illness.

"First, I'm not dying. Well I am as we all are a little bit each day, but nothing that I know of is going to carry me out right now. So you can stop holding your breath." Madeline watched as her daughter's shoulders sunk with relief. Seeing that Cherish also had tears, she snatched a box of tissues from the kitchen counter and sat them in front of her. "You'll probably need several of these."

Cherish furrowed her brow. "I thought you said you're not sick. What's happening, Mom? What could you possibly have to tell me that would make me continue to cry? Is it Tierra? Is she okay? She's safe isn't she?"

Madeline nodded. "The mind is funny in how it'll allow you to pack things away in the back. Lets you redesign the story so to speak. Been a long time since I've rummaged through these mental boxes." Images of herself as a young woman laboring in a hospital room with no husband to hold her hand, took over her vision. Her eyes reddened when she pictured herself bringing Cherish home to an empty house, only to be visited after midnight by Mr. Baylock. There as a squeezing on her heart when she recalled the way she carried her daughter to the church alter while the congregation prayed over her.

When Madeline inhaled, she took in all that was, everything that existed, and one more time, exhaling as she surrendered to the crashing of worlds. "Let me just spit this out because making you run this gamut of emotions isn't fair either." She held Cherish's hand. "Remember when you were little and you'd ask about your father, but then I'd avoid answering? I'd get so irate and point out all things you ought to be grateful for rather than asking about what you were missing. Eventually you steered clear of the topic. Now that I think of it, it was pretty mean." She squinted. "Evil almost. I mean to deny you even a photo to fuel your imagination."

Cherish nodded. "But I got over it. Whomever he was, whatever happened, I realized it hurt too deep for you to share. Over the years I became so enthralled with my own sagas, I stopped wondering about him."

Tightening her grip around Cherish's knuckles, Madeline focused on the table. Echoes of her warnings to Mr. Baylock crept through her mind. *What will she think of you, of me? She can't know. It's better this way.* If she could avoid her daughter's eyes, she could possibly miss the onset of the repugnance she was sure would follow. "Mr. Baylock is your father. There, I said it."

All was quiet. Frozen by shock, Cherish stared as if she had yet to hear the news of her father's existence. Madeline could feel her daughter's fists hardening under the cover of Madeline's fingers. Her own hands were shaking, but she didn't want to let go. Cherish was never violent, but there was no telling how the body would react to this kind of crushing reality.

Suddenly, Madeline's hands were empty as Cherish reclaimed hers. *Come on Maddy, at the very least you have to look her in her eyes. You owe her so much more than that.* With trepidation, Madeline lifted her head.

Forgoing the tissues Madeline provided for her, Cherish allowed her tears to puddle the table. Her eyes were wide, fingers clutching the corners of her cardigan. The water behind Madeline's eyes knew not how to comfort. So they flowed in company to the anguish streaming down Cherish's cheeks.

The air in Cherish's lungs was too much and yet not enough. She gasped, fighting for her words. "How, how, but why... He was here, Mom! He was here. In my life, buying school clothes, helping with homework... Why? What for? Why make me feel like charity, like he was the closest thing I had to a father? He was my father," she roared.

Madeline winced. Only once had she heard Cherish's voice so loud and that was when demanding doctors hurry with issuing her an epidural. Then she was able to soothe Cherish with gentle touches and assurance of all being okay. Now she wasn't sure enough of the future to know what to offer.

"I fell in love with my neighbor's husband. It was wrong and we knew it. We just had this insatiable appetite for each other. I still have the letters we wrote to each other, every one of them breaking it off for the good of his marriage and really our salvation."

The volcanic emotions bubbling in Cherish's esophagus was at its peak. She jumped for her chair. "We went to her funeral!" Her voice quieted, "Yet I can't even imagine her face. It's like I don't even remember his wife! She's insignificant in my memory." Tension narrowed her words and stressed her tone. "How could you reduce her like that? I'm going to be sick." Bile made its way up like lava and emptied onto the kitchen floor. Cherish dropped to the floor beside it, on her knees, emptying more of it.

Madeline rushed to her daughter and wrapped her arms around her. "Cherish I'm sorry. It's my greatest sin to have violated that woman so. But it was a blessing because I had you and for the hope that you would be greater than I is why I tried to raise you in the church. I hated myself and wanted you to be everything I wasn't. But my silence, it didn't help you, just as yours isn't helping Tierra. It's why I keep pushing to get to the bottom of this Jackson Trent thing."

Cherish's coughing slowed. Rage continued its whirlwind as her cheeks reddened and saliva stuck. "After what you just told me, you're still judging me?" She shoved the old woman aside. "Judging what I did?" Picking herself up from the floor, she continued her rant. "I honored Brandon. Gave him the child he always wanted, but knew he could never have. What you did is different. Don't compare me to you. My whole life you lied to me. So adamant about showing Mr. Baylock respect. What about me? Did you respect me? You stripped me of the right to be able to call my father, Daddy."

Unable to stand on her own, Madeline grabbed for the chair leg. The way her daughter looked down upon her, with disgust, hatred, she knew she'd have to find a way to get herself upright. With all her might she pulled, using her words to give her strength. "I don't deny we've made treacherous mistakes. However, it doesn't excuse repeating them." Fully erect, she caught her breath. "You can be angry with me and never talk to me again. I've earned that. But you know who hasn't earned it? Tierra. It doesn't take a rocket scientist to figure out your bouts of silence are merely hiding places for your guilt. I'm telling you that I recognize that conflicted self-loathe because I've felt it, daily. You think I don't understand? Maybe I don't. But neither does Tierra and she at least deserves an explanation. Just as you do."

As if fleeing an assailant, Cherish darted out of the kitchen. Clumsily she jerked open the coat closet, grabbed her coat, and headed out of the front door. One arm in a sleeve, struggling to capture the other, she began her trek down the street.

Madeline decided not to attempt to chase Cherish. There was no good she would be able to do by running until her knees gave out or her heart stopped beating. All that she had said was enough for an eternity of Cherish's un-forgiveness. Instead she reached for the phone posted on the kitchen wall.

"Hi Randy. Yeah I'm all right. I had to tell Cherish about us. Of course she's upset. Livid, actually." She held her head while listening.

"I wouldn't advise it, but if you want to try you can. Knowing her, it'll take a few hours before she's home. She'll wander a bit." Madeline glanced at the clock over the kitchen sink. It read 6:16. She was overdue to start dinner. "In the meantime, can you come over and help me mop? She done spit up and all her guts are all over the floor."

15 WHAT I GAVE TO YOU

Cherish sat at the edge of her bed. She stared at her feet under the dim light. Her toes hidden by the hood of her slippers, while the bases of her feet remained exposed. Rattling the window was the December wind. It seemed to be warning her that Christmas would soon be here and unwrapping her truths was no longer something she could avoid.

****
****

"I'm sorry. I shouldn't have kissed you." Although he had straightened his lean, Jackson still had her hand. Twiddling with her fingers, she could tell he was trying to let go, but couldn't make himself believe that he wanted to.

"Your lips, they're nice." Cherish touched her own lips, sealing in the memory of his. Her fingers still intertwined with his, she couldn't pull away. She waged her tongue across her bottom lip, hoping to re-taste him. Mint still detectable, she sucked, taking it all in.

They were alone in his cousin's house, waiting for her to return. The three of them had enjoyed movies and days of laughter. Cherish wasn't accustomed to having friends and she took to Lanaeya upon introduction. Jackson was right to claim Lanaeya as his sister. If she hadn't known the origin of their relation, Cherish would've assumed the same. They poked fun at each other, argued over trivial things like untimely channel changes, and agreed on mostly everything related to sports.

Set to watch another James Bond portrayal in Lanaeya's basement, the trio decided to order pizza. Opting for the best Pizzeria in the neighborhood meant delivery wouldn't be available so naturally since Lanaeya was the only one with a car, she volunteered to go get it.

Maybe she knew the kiss would happen. Maybe she didn't, but time knew that if left alone, restraint would be impossible.

Cherish held tight to Jackson's hand. He pulled her closer to him. They sat on the torn leather sofa, enveloped into each other, trying not to think about anything. Until she turned to him.

His cologne filled her airwaves. Her knee crawled up his thigh. He embraced her torso. Again, their lips met. Magnets unable to resist each other's allure, their tongues collided. In tune with the song of feverish blood, their bodies swayed, pulled, pushed.

The moment he saw her in his apartment, searching for Brandon, Jackson envisioned his hands gripping her wild curls, in his mouth her breasts. Fulfilling his lusts, he carried her to the floor. Her legs secured around his hips, he breathed her in.

Skin to skin, she wanted to leap into him. His hair tickling her navel. He bowed at her waist.

She opened her path and allowed him to sample her fruit. Her heart raced with each shiver. When he mounted, she did not contest, but welcomed him in. She swirled her hips to keep his rhythm. Tangled, they explored, hoping to never find a way out.

****

****

Cherish removed her feet from her slippers. On her left foot, she could see the nail on the biggest toe was cracking. It had been a long time since she used polish or even allowed anyone to care for them.

On the nightstand, stood a picture of Brandon holding his company football trophy. He had led the team to victory three years in a row. His smile was wide. She picked it up and traced the details of his face. She sighed. "I still don't know how you were able to love me so."

Recalling the day they married, Cherish could still hear Brandon's vows. *If you let me, I'll love you forever. On your good days, your bad days, your days of ambition, and even your days of doubt, you will always be loved.* He then placed the wedding band on her finger. The judge smiled at the two of them. Brandon's father nodded as to say, "It is done." Cherish's mother chanted, "Amen, amen, and amen."

In this one moment alone, she decided to be honest with herself. There was joy in both memories. Passion in the first that would forever redden her cheeks and clam her thighs. However, the second memory was what gave her what she reckoned to be a real family. Tierra in her belly, a husband dedicated to being her protector and a father to her child, everything she yearned for as a young girl.

Now with her protector gone, her passion was coming to haunt. Still as remarkably handsome as he was back then, it seemed even more imperative that she kept away from Jackson Trent. Tierra may never forgive her as she was struggling to consider the forgiveness her own mother hoped for. Turning over the events in her mind, she said aloud, "What a funny thing, the truth. We wish for it as though it would equip us to come to resolutions. But once it spills, no one wants to clean up the mess."

16 IN MY HOUSE

From the top stair leading to her grandmother's porch, the scent of oatmeal raisin cookies floated through Tierra's nostrils. They were her favorite and after scoping out every bakery she came across, she decided no one made them as warm, and as soft as her grandmother did. She inhaled as set her suitcases down.

Madeline wrung her hands dry in the sink and hurried for the door. She'd been counting down the days to Tierra's Christmas vacation. When Tierra finally called her after the last spat, Madeline was relieved. *Good. Now if Cherish can get to talking to me too, maybe we can all get this healing started. Now you're wishing for a Christmas miracle, Maddie.* She chuckled.

Beaming with excitement, Madeline opened the door. "Oh my, Tierra! You look so good. Your shoulders broaden, perhaps?" She squealed while Tierra carried her bags inside. "It's so good to see you." She hugged Tierra tightly and took her coat. Tierra plopped down in her favorite spot by the living room couch. "I'm sorry Mr. Baylock couldn't come get you." Madeline paused. Tierra didn't flinch. *Of course, Cherish hasn't said anything. She hardly talks to the girl.* "He's sorry too. His hip has been acting up and I thought you'd probably be safer if he didn't drive, you know what I mean? Remind me to give you the money back for the cab." She joined Tierra in the living room.

Tierra looked around. The olive-green couch was surprisingly uncovered. The matching armchair was also bare. There was always an armchair at the other end of the room as well, but it was no longer the beige one she was accustomed to. It was now gray with images of tiny green potted plants throughout. "Wow! Living room looks brand new. You find a sugar daddy or something, Gran? Or is Mr. Trent's money still finding its way in your mailbox?"

"Oh, stop that! You can't play nice just for a moment? Sheesh! The plastic started to make my kneecaps sweat, so I got rid of it. That's the same old chair over there. I just had it reupholstered. I figured that by now I'm old enough to enjoy the furniture I preserved. Aren't I? Well, I don't know. I might be speaking from Mr. Baylock's tongue." Watching for Tierra's reaction, Madeline eased herself into an armchair. Still nothing.

Tierra noticed how the centered coffee table still held her grandmother's hefty, tattered Bible. Next to it was a framed black and white picture of Tierra's parents donned in party hats, holding Tierra as a toddler up in the air to blow out the candles on her birthday cake.

"You look too contemplative. Rest. You can bring your cases up to your room later on. Tell me about school. The semester is over now. How do you think you did?"

Tierra examined her grandmother. The woman looked more comfortable than Tierra had ever seen her. Aside from sitting on the uncovered chair, something even Cherish had probably never seen, Tierra tried to figure out why the woman was so different.

"Take those sunglasses off. You're in the house."

Nope, she's still the same. Tierra removed her shades. She grabbed for her gold metallic shoulder bag and retrieved a brown signature case. After placing the glasses inside, she repositioned the bag between her and the inner arm of the sofa. Her grandmother watched as she took her time. Attempting to get more comfortable, Tierra unfastened the buttons on her cardigan.

"Cashmere?"

Tierra nodded though offered no explanation. She hoped her grandmother wouldn't ask for one. *I knew I shouldn't' have gotten rid of those old clothes. I should've just packed them to come here. Now the Captain of Runaway Imagination is going to ask me all kinds of questions like if I'm selling drugs or something.* With each of the buttons unfastened, Tierra carefully laid her sweater on the cushion next to her. She then straightened her back. Mr. Cherry had schooled that sitting erect gave her more control of her appearance, which in turn would make her appear more alluring.

"Well, this is certainly a new you. Nails all done up. You cut your hair. Looks good. I've been trying to get you to sit up straight for most of your life. Glad to see you're caring about your posture. Your bag looks new. You've been shopping? I didn't think I was sending you enough money to afford all of this! Are you eating? Well, I know you're eating. You look healthier than me, that's for sure. Working out too. I hope you're not into that body building stuff. Keep soft-like. You're still a young lady. You should be saving any money that's extra, though, not shopping. That's not what I send it to you for."

Tierra remained quiet. It was hard keeping her thoughts from seeping through her lips, but she knew it was necessary. *Don't nobody need that damn money she keeps sending. Hell, I'd send it back if she wouldn't ask so many questions. She always has questions? Can't she just be happy I look well. Damn!* She tried to think of a believable lie. Her foot tapped the carpet with the mounting pressure. Madeline wasn't the type to ask questions and be okay with not getting a response.

"Oh, I got a job at the library on campus. I didn't tell you?"

"No, you didn't. That's nice. The library is a great place for you to work. You probably get even more study time in that way. Smart girl. How many hours do you work? I hope not too much. Well it can't be cause you working on that voluptuous figure. You know your studying is more important than all this stuff," she alluded to

Tierra's sweater and bag. "I send you money. You don't have to overwork."

"I think I probably would've told you last time I was here, but you know…" Tierra rolled her eyes. Recalling her name in Jackson's handwriting was giving her a headache. Michelle had convinced her to see her grandmother for the holiday. Tierra would've preferred to stick around the club and earn some extra cash. It was anyone's guess what circumstance she'd come home to. But Michelle was right, *Girl, your grandmother is old. You want to be mad with her when you lose her? She fouled out but you can't take away her Christmas.* It still didn't mean that she couldn't use the incident as a means to keep her grandmother from getting on her case too much. Regret was a handy tool if handled properly.

"Enough of the attitude, Tierra. I just don't want you working to get all this stuff and lose sight of what's important. You can be upset with me over Jackson. I get that and respect your feelings. Still I want to make sure my granddaughter is taking care of herself."

Tierra tapped her foot.

Madeline took note of her granddaughter's tapping agitation. Foreseeing the visit ending in the manner of the previous, she decidedly lightened the mood. "All right, Tierra. I know you just got in. You have every right to be independent and make your own money without your old grandmother worrying all over you, I suppose. You're a good girl! Let's go into the kitchen and have some cookies."

Tierra was relieved for the reprieve. Following Madeline into the kitchen, she eyed the liquor cabinet. *Tonight's unwind shall be great and well deserved. Cause this woman right here… I swear she's gotten more annoying than I remember.*

Being the "good Christian woman," Madeline was, there was no chance Tierra would be able to drink without her grandmother's sensitive nose and subsequent chastising. She patted her pocket. If she took one of the tablets she bought from Corinne before she left, it might take the edge off. Still, she figured if she was going to dodge anymore of her grandmother's questioning, she ought to not take the chance of being too relaxed. She might just tell the woman all she didn't want to know.

At the kitchen table, Madeline placed four oatmeal cookies on a porcelain plate that depicted a small red house atop a hill of grass. She poured Tierra a glass of milk, stirred in some chocolate syrup, and placed it next to the plate. She then pulled out Tierra's chair as if Tierra was still a toddler with not enough strength to do it herself.

The soft cookies danced their sugar around Tierra's tongue. She chewed slowly, letting the sweetness of the raisins nestle in the crowns of her teeth. One gulp of milk was all it took to get the remaining hints of cinnamon to reach the back of her throat with one last frolic before it all went down.

"Gran, these are so good!" It was Tierra's attempt at making peace. The previous moments had soured her taste buds, but the warmth of the cookies reminded her of her grandmother's intent. *She's just trying to be good...for everyone.*

Madeline blushed. "Oh Tierra, don't exaggerate. I know they're your favorite. I can make some for you to take back to school if you like. Just remind me after the New Year. I think I'll have to re-up on the vanilla extract."

Recalling Mr. Cherry's warning about the danger in her love for baked goods, Tierra dropped the remainder of the first cookie back onto the plate. "No, don't put yourself out like that. I don't want to get fat anyway. I shouldn't even eat these four. The half I had was plenty."

Stunned, Madeline stopped fussing through the cabinets. She did notice Tierra looked slimmer around the waist, but she assumed the girl wouldn't deny her favorite treat. In the teal sweater dress, Tierra was much shapelier than when she left for school back in August. Her hips were more defined, her breasts appeared firmer. Madeline considered their last argument might've distracted her from noticing before. *Tierra never worried about her weight before. It fluctuated from time to time but she always seemed okay with that. I wonder who's got her minding such things. She better not be trying to redesign herself for a boy.*

"Since when are you worried about your weight? You look beautiful to me, always! I hope you're not letting those college boys make you think you need to be too aware of yourself. You're not built to look like those stick-thin models, Tierra. You're father's a football player. If he were here, he'd snap the neck of any man making you question your size. You're a beautiful size!"

The mention of her father caused Tierra to clench her jaw. Speaking of him as if he were still alive indicated that Madeline was referring to Jackson. Tierra took a deep breath. *Well, she did say if he were here so maybe she's talking about my real dad. I sure wish he were here right now.* Tierra was back to tapping her foot. "My father's dead so there's no necks to snap."

My goodness, so easy does Brandon's death roll off her tongue? What is it with this girl? I knew I should've had her start school here. She's off on her own and now talking like she's somebody's woman. Her age might be adult according to the government, but this attitude is all child. Madeline was careful not to speak her mind. The Christmas break was only a few short weeks and she didn't want to spend the opening moments pitted against Tierra. Grabbing Tierra by the shoulders, she looked into her granddaughter's sparkling eyes. "I understand you are entitled to look as good as you think you should. It's okay as long as it comes from what you want. You don't have to go out of your way to please anyone else's eye, that's all I was saying. Just be pleasing to God. You can do that by just doing His will!"

"Okay, I got it! I'm good like these cookies are good." Tierra forced a smile. The presence of mind to know her grandmother would be looking to read something into Tierra's newfound boldness, Tierra looked away. In the past her grandmother would always be able to tell when she was avoiding her emotions. Discernment is what she called it. This time though, it was for her grandmother's own good Tierra would bite her tongue.

Every holiday couldn't be marked with a spat. It seemed so out of place in her house. With as many years as they fought against Cherish's silence together, Tierra didn't want to fight on an opposing team. "Look at that. My stomach decided to eat all four. I guess I'm not as disciplined as I hoped."

Madeline grinned, but remained uneasy. The Tierra that sat before her was much more combative than the child she helped raise. She tried not to glare while Tierra devoured her cookies and chugged her milk. The girl then put her plate in the sink and left it for Madeline to wash. Correctly reading the lines in Madeline's forehead and hand perched on her hip, Tierra rounded back to the sink then squired dish detergent on a sponge.

"So Gran, what are we doing we doing for Christmas? Mommy showing up this year? You know she's hit or miss. Are you cooking the usual turkey dinner or you getting fancy this year?"

Finally breaking her trance, Madeline began using her hand to sweep crumbs off the table. "Actually, Tierra, I'm not cooking this year. I ordered some food from Miss Maggie's catering company. They are going to bring the food over on Christmas Eve and we'll spend the day at your house with your mom."

"Oh?"

Madeline paused. Thinking of all the things there were to come when Tierra found that Mr. Baylock was her grandfather (if she didn't already know) or that Jackson would be at Christmas dinner, Madeline was growing tired. *It's like I got to keep running from these children and all their feelings. We got to go through some hard falls to pick ourselves up and I can't keep shielding them from bruising their knees.*

"It's probably going to be a fiasco but I'm tired of dancing around it." Madeline wiped the table. She then put Tierra's chair back in. "Mr. Baylock is going to be there and if Cherish hasn't already told you about why she's so pissy with me lately, it's because I finally told her the truth. He's your grandfather. Mr. Baylock is your mother's father. There. Now we all know everyone's sin."

The sound of porcelain crashing against the kitchen tile was as loud as Madeline's thumping heart. She hadn't planned on spitting it out like that, but reasoned that sitting Cherish down to tell her the news didn't pan out the way she wanted. What did it matter anyway? She had been trying to preserve her relationships with both her daughter and granddaughter and they still ended up feeling as though she slid knives through their backs. Why would they pretend like everything was normal? It wasn't normal. There was too much unsaid. They hadn't spent Christmas in the house where Tierra grew up in six years. Admittedly, having Jackson there would be odd but Madeline wanted Cherish and Tierra to be on their own territory. That was least she could gift them.

Madeline dutifully grabbed the broom and began sweeping up the pieces of porcelain. "I'm guessing you haven't talked to her any more than she's talked to you over the years. I figured she'd at least ring you, seeing as she might be feeling something akin to what you've been dealing with. And while you've got eyebrows all furrowed and I'm catching pieces of your jaw up in my broom I might as well tell you I invited Jackson to dinner too." There was a tiny piece of dish that fell beneath the sink cabinet. She gritted her teeth as she shoved the broom under, attempting to dig it out.

Cheeks a-flame and her voice cracking, Tierra pounced on the opportunity to share her piece. "You act like my mother and I don't have any say about who comes into our home, our lives. You often ask what's gotten into us, but what the hell has gotten into you?"

"Tierra Genelle Proper, now you stop right there! Don't you ever fix your mouth to curse me. I'd slap fire out of you if I wasn't aware of all that indignation you carryin', like you waiting for a chance to whoop me. As for your mother, she's not talking about it, Tierra. Part of that is my fault. Yes, it's horrible what I did to her with not sharing who her father is. Just like it's horrible that she kept from Jackson that he had a child. Didn't even give him the chance to see you. I thought I was shielding her from being like me and she ended up sinning my sin two times over. If we continue this way, who knows what will be on your docket when you cross the line? Cherish may be your mother, but she is my child and you are hers. I refuse to keep recoloring the lines for the sake of softer blows. It hasn't helped any of us. You running around with money from God knows where, thinking that a couple dollars make you a woman, Cherish talking then not talking half the time, I'm sick of it."

Tears welled in Tierra's eyes. "Both of you are so damn selfish! For years she's been wallowing in her pain like no one else has any. And then I find out that maybe it's not pain, it's guilt. She was out there being Queen Harlot and my dad took pity on her."

Slap! Madeline had heard enough. Regardless of Cherish's actions, she would not allow her child to stand in her presence and disrespect Cherish so. "Keep talking and you'll give me the strength to beat your ass."

Tierra held her cheek. "Really? You smacking me now for speaking the truth? I'm not fighting for my mother's honor, just as she has never defended my peace. Daddy died and she abandoned me. Curled up into her mind, cowardly. This whole time she's been ducking a nineteen-year-old spring fling. Yeah, I did the math." She stormed into the living room and grabbed her sweater. "This was a mistake. I'm going back."

Madeline limped behind Tierra. "Tierra! Going back where? Don't walk away like that."

Tierra focused on gathering her suitcases. *She should feel grateful. No gifts to buy. I'll send her something and get my own. But I'm not playing this game. She wants to all of a sudden fight for men's rights and my mother's name, that's her choice. I'm not doing it though.*

Madeline tried placing herself between Tierra and the front door. "Tierra stop! This can't be our holiday. I love you. I just want us to not have any of these family secrets. Honestly, it's for the sake of your future and your children's future."

Tierra shouted, "Seriously, what world are you living in? You talking about children and I haven't even got a doggone boyfriend. You think I'm going to follow in yours and Mommy's footsteps? I won't. Neither of you went to school. I'm already different. So now there's no need to worry. Now let me go."

Inside Tierra felt like all her cells were jumping and bumping into each other. There was a rocket in her veins and if she didn't walk out of there soon, it was going to shoot out of her mouth. She had already said more than she had ever dared to say to her grandmother's face. Her "Gran" was always spouting Bible verses, aiming to convince Tierra that anyone would be considered prime for Satan's army if they didn't build their entire lives around Proverbs. During her last two visits she was finding her grandmother's act to be a farce.

"How dare you! You have no idea how your mother suffered when Brandon died. Did he love her past her mistakes, yes, just as love requires. I'm not asking for your forgiveness for entertaining a truth Brandon wanted uncovered. He knew the truth and if you're so much into honoring him you'd be trying to figure why he'd reach out to Jackson in the first place. I'd assume it was to make amends for his own guilt about keeping the man's child from him. As for Mr. Baylock and I, you and Cherish can judge if you must. That's my cross to bear and I'm most blessed to still have him as my partner to carry the load with. I'm going to do everything I can to square that away with Cherish, but you thinking that our mistakes gives you right to talk to anyone like you haven't been provided for everyday of your life is way far out of line. So, you know, now that I think of it, if you want to run back to the school that everybody's money but yours pays for, then you do that. If education is what you're running to, God bless you." She stepped aside.

Tierra's face was drenched with tears. Her heart told her that life would never be the same after this moment. No more was she covered under her grandmother's love and grace. There was no taking back anything that was said. The thought of Jackson Trent coming between them pained her chest. "God bless you too, Gran. You let him change us."

Madeline spoke calmly, but her finger wasn't any less pointed. "If you don't want to see your father, you're old enough to decide that. I'll be here. I hope wherever you think you're going will welcome you with open arms cause it's a cold world out there. You don't want your family, despite how convoluted we might be, then fine. I know these streets more than you think an old lady might. When you get your head clear, cause I know you will, I'll be waiting for you. But when you come back, know that this is still my house and you will respect me in it!"

Tierra pushed her suitcases out of the door. Just as her foot left the top stair, she heard the door shut behind her. The sound caused a jerk in her rhythm. The outside air seemed colder than usual as it passed through her lungs. The wind blew, intending to freeze her tears. She'd have to find some other way to do the same for her heart.

17 OUT OF CLASS

Bleep, bleep bleep! It was four in the afternoon. Tierra awakened. The motel room she had spent the last two nights in was dark as midnight. Hallway lights peeked from the beneath the door. Airplane bottles of vodka scattered the lint-speckled carpet.

"Who the hell set the alarm clock for the afternoon in a doggone motel? Who checks out at four?" Tierra mashed the buttons on the side of the clock until she found the one that quieted the alarm. She grabbed for a pillow to bury her head then thought better of it. If the dorms had been opened for the holidays she would've opted to stay there. It occurred to her to call Michelle, but then she'd be probed to give the details of her fallout with Gran. *Michelle running away from everything her mother wants for her. She has no idea what it's like to have a mother who you've seen every day but still didn't know.*

Finding a place to stay wasn't as easy as Tierra thought it'd be. She went to several of the nicer hotels near campus. They each wanted a credit card on file and after several neck-snapping altercations with management, she gave in to checking into the only place that would take cash as the deposit.

You know, I don't want to be sad anymore. My mother is a sad somebody, but that's who she chooses to be. I don't want to be like that. So I'm not. I'm my own woman, free from Gran's rules on how to live and I don't need to live in the shadows of my mother's secret life. I have my own.

She took a business card from her wallet and began dialing the number scribbled on the back. "Hello, Mr. Leonard?" She giggled. "I'm sorry, Michael."

■■■■■■■■■■■■■■■■■■■■■■■■■■■■■■■■■■■■■

At 8:00 PM Tierra was stepping out of the shower. Wrapped in a towel she scurried to answer the knock at the door. "Who is it?"

"Michael," said the voice on the other side of the door.

As he strolled in, Mr. Leonard held up a brown paper bag. "I bought champagne. Honestly, I didn't know what else to bring. I've never done this before."

"Done what?"

"This. Meet with a stripper. I…I…I mean a student. Well you are a …. I don't know what I'm saying. Can you tell I'm nervous? You're just so beautiful."

"Yeah, the bashful smile kind of gave it away." Suddenly, Tierra realized that she was still in her towel. "I'm sorry. Let me get dressed. I didn't even realize…" She started to call the rest of her sentence out from the bathroom, but stopped as she assumed he wouldn't hear her anyway.

Mr. Leonard surveyed the room. The floral bedspread was in place as if Tierra had not slept there, but her suitcases looked rummaged through as if she had. The pillows were dented. Her head had definitely rested on them. Unsure if he would seem too forward by sitting on the bed, he chose to sit in the recliner in the corner.

Tierra re-emerged fully dressed. She wore a pair of form fitting jeans and a black top with lace that hinted at her undergarments, but failed to actually reveal any. Her hair was swept into a bun. She sat at the edge of the bed hunched over, looking through the suitcase that held her four new pairs of shoes.

"I hope you don't think I'm trying to seduce you for a better grade. I think I actually did well in your class so I should be okay, right? Just thought it might be safe to hang out now that the semester is over and you're officially not my professor anymore."

"I'm flattered, happy actually that you called. Hey, I brought the champagne, didn't I? Might not be such a bad thing if you did intend to seduce me. I might like it." He took up a spot on the edge of the bed next to Tierra.

Deciding on what shoe to wear took a backseat to her recalculation of the man seated beside her. He removed the champagne from the paper bag. *He just wants to sleep with me. Well of course he does, Tierra. He's seen you naked. You think he knows that you're a virgin wishing upon a star for a boyfriend? No, stupid! So now how do I ask him to leave?*

Mr. Leonard searched the room. Finding the tray that held two coffee mugs with packets of coffee stuffed inside he seemed disappointed. "No glasses? Well, I guess we can use these." He poured Tierra a mug's full of champagne and offered it to her. Despite her apprehensiveness, he shoved it closer until she took it.

Nervously, she noted, "Sure seems like a lot when you pour it in here."

"It is, but you don't have to drink it all. Your knees are shaking. Am I off-putting? Would you like me to leave?"

This was the out. Her grandmother always said there'd be one. That one moment right before you make a bad decision that the good Lord gives you a glimmer of the exit. *If I said so, he'd leave and that would be that. But then what? Forever the tease I'd be, I guess. And if I had to lose my virginity he sure isn't the worst looking guy to lose it to. Or I could sit here and be alone, twisted off of this…* She sipped. What tasted like bitter mouthwash attacked her tongue and bullied its way to the back of her throat. Eyes squeezed together, she fought to overcome her instinct to spit it up. *Is that what champagne tastes like?*

Mr. Leonard removed the bottle's label as he poured a cup for himself. "I admit it's not the fanciest. Not much I can do on a teacher's salary. I haven't made tenure."

Tierra studied her cup. *Should I take another sip? I'm going to need so much more than this if I'm going to let him do this. God did bless him in the looks department, but why does he seem so lame now? Ordinarily, he seems brilliant. Can you imagine losing my virginity to my teacher? Unreal. Michelle would do back flips over this story.*

Taking Tierra by the hand, Mr. Leonard pulled her up to him. He held her to his chest and swayed with her. Nestling his chin upon her shoulder, his breaths were heavy and too close to her ear. "You're a very beautiful woman. The way you dance is quite thrilling, really." Softly he nibbled at her collarbone.

Tierra gulped the harsh liquid lingering in her cup. He pressed himself closer to her. Woozy faster than she anticipated, her head started to feel like she'd been hit with a four by four. The side of her face was wet. She touched it but blurred vision made it hard to tell the color of the stream. Tierra stumbled. The room darkened. Confused, she sought Mr. Leonard's eyes for clarity. Hs stared at her, awaiting something, she wasn't sure what.

What did he put in that cup? Tierra attempted blinking in rapid succession. Hoping she could force immediate sobriety, she shook her head. The room moved in slow motion. "Did you dru…" Her head was heavy. She felt herself being carried to the bed. He laid her down. She fell back into his guidance. She wanted to ask the question again, but couldn't bring her mouth to form the words.

"Don't worry. I promise I'll be gentle, Miss Tierra. It's just a little something to take the edge off. I figured you might be nervous. Now, you don't have to be. Just give in to what your body tells you. You're going to love it."

No. I'm not ready. What is he doing? I was going to… No, get off of me. There was no cry. There was no scream. There was only the protest in her mind. Her face shoved in a pillow, he mounted her. Something like a worm tickled her pelvis. It was soft and flapped around, searching for an opening. She thought to pull herself away. Her arms numb, weightless, no will to fight. Cheap corner store alcohol ravaged her nostrils.

Decidedly turning her over, Michael Leonard dangled his member over Tierra's head, gyrating and grinning as if she had invited the movements. Skin thick and clammed was hardening with each bump against her cheeks and chin. Shoving himself into her mouth, he sighed with relief. "Oh my…"

Tierra thought she'd gag. Pungent sweat coupled with the salt of her tears poured bitters for her swallow. Still she took it in, drooling saliva, which he accepted as lubrication.

He bit his knuckles. "Ooh, warm just as I thought it'd be." Picking up the pace of his bucks, he convulsed until relieved.

With no control over her muscles, the fluid spilled from her mouth, demanding she swallowed the bit sliding to the back of her tongue. Ejecting himself, he leapt to his feet. As if following a planned list of execution, he quickly wiped his member on the towel she once had wrapped around her.

With her jeans stripped down to her knees, her underwear held to the side, he dragged Tierra to the edge of the bed. As he parted her thighs he worked his way in. The force pushing through her hymen burned. Inside her head she could hear her screams for him to stop, but still her vocal chords were empty of sound. He jabbed. The sound of ripping permeated her ears. Finally her opening had let down its guard. No longer did she try to hold her breath. Something like pee rushed her vagina.

Feeling Tierra's opening give up resistance, Mr. Leonard's thrusts became steady, less impatient. His touches became gentle. Slowly, he pulled out. As if motivated to stimulate, he dove his face into the lips of her cave, forgetting that it was he who bombarded its closure.

Tierra's skin burns dulled. A tickling tingle developed near her rear. After much failure, her eyes finally gave in to tears. Shame battered her soul. For the welcoming her body now felt baffled her. *He's raping me! It hurts. I know it does. But why does it feel like...* A waterfall emptied down her thighs. Her eyes were still to him, unable to shut or look away.

Mr. Leonard yanked himself out of her and drizzled his milk atop her face. He zippered up, then kissed her cheek. As a courtesy, he used her towel to wipe clear her eyes and mouth. From his pocket he produced, five hundred dollar bills. He folded it and placed in under the nightstand lamp. Leaving the cheap champagne behind, he let himself out. Had he turned back, he would've known Tierra was regaining feeling in her limbs, puking over the tattered carpet with hopes of going numb again.

18 SHEDDING LIGHT

"Mom, I'm ready to talk." Cherish had been out on Madeline's porch for nearly half an hour pacing. Embarrassed at how she reacted to the news of Mr. Baylock as her father, she considered an apology. However, she reasoned that she deserved to have an emotion. It was a cruel secret and despite her mother's plight, it was something she shouldn't have kept from her. Still, what she was doing to Jackson was also inexcusable. If any of them were to have any peace, they'd have to begin to pick up the pieces of what was and decide how to move forward.

"I thought you'd never speak to me again." Madeline stood in the doorway behind the screen. "Not sure if you want to come in. Mr. Baylock, well your father, is here."

Although a sound that would take some getting used to, the reference to someone as her father made Cherish giddy. As a child she hoped for the day a man would walk into their home and claim her as his sorely missed princess. He'd apologize for abandoning her, promising to never commit such a sin again. She'd forgive him and share with him her bubblegum, her love for puzzles, and they'd laugh at her favorite television programs. Now she was here on her mother's stoop, recalling the man who she presumed was a caring neighbor who placed himself as a stand in. He did do puzzles with her, took her to the store to pick which bubblegum she wanted, and he'd make her promise to do her homework before sitting down in front of the television.

"My father, yes that he is. I'd like to come in."

From the armchair in which he waited once he heard her voice, Mr. Baylock stood to welcome his daughter inside. A strong elderly man, his hands shook. Cherish embraced him. They held each other, rocking from side to side. She wiped his tears.

"You made mistakes, but haven't we all? You made a mess... as did I. Still, you were there for me and for that I'm grateful."

Madeline was amazed at Cherish's movement to forgive. She watched as Mr. Baylock helped Cherish remove her coat. Madeline took it from him to hang on the wooden garment tree he had bought her for Christmas. Taking her time draping the coat, she whispered a "thank you" to God. *You've never forsaken me. Even when I've turned my back to you, my cup is still overflowing. Thank you, Lord.*

As her mother rejoined them in the living room, Cherish prepared herself to tell her story. She took a deep breath and asked her mother to sit next to her. "What I'm going to admit, I've never said aloud." She couldn't say much more than that without the water from her eyes oozing out like streams down a mountainside. Mr. Baylock raised up to get her a tissue, but she hopped up and grabbed his wrist. "Not even to wipe my tears do I want you to leave right now. You allowed me to have pieces of your truth and now I'm going to share a piece of mine."

Agreeing to stay, Mr. Baylock took his seat. He glanced at Madeline and could see that the anticipation of a revelation had her anxious. She rubbed her palms together and pressed them against her flour-ridden house-skirt. He wanted to tell her it would be all right and he'd be there for support no matter the circumstance. He settled for nodding.

Cherish held her mother's hand. She smoothed over the wrinkles. A tight squeeze from Madeline let Cherish know that it was safe to confide. "Seems most appropriate to just answer the question I guess. Could Jackson Trent be Tierra's father? When I first found myself pregnant, I told myself no. It was not possible that anyone other than Brandon was the father of the seed that pulsed about on the sonogram screen."

Madeline held her fingers to her lips as they trembled. She recalled the way Brandon gazed at baby Tierra in the hospital. He named her. With tears in his eyes he kissed her forehead and vowed to love her.

"As a young girl, I really liked Brandon. Over the years I grew to love him and everything he stood for. He was the greatest man I knew, will ever know, and I was grateful that he loved me."

Mr. Baylock shifted in his chair. There was a contradiction coming; a contrast that he identified with. He, too, loved his wife. He provided for her every need before she passed. However, Madeline intoxicated him with merely her smile. Of course, Cherish may not have struggled for the length of time he did, but he knew the afflictions of having a conflicted heart.

"Mama, remember my friend Lanaeya down the street?" Cherish remained focused on her mother's hands. "So, happens that she and Jackson are cousins. If you recall, I stopped answering her calls and would tell you to tell her I wasn't home when she came by? I didn't want her to see me pregnant. She knew the truth."

"The day it happened, Jackson and I, she could tell. We picked at our pizza, the same pie that we were all starving for, and we could only chew in small pieces while avoiding looking into each other's eyes. Lanaeya never said anything. In fact I think she liked the two of us together. But she knew. You couldn't spend more than five minutes near the two of us and not know."

Madeline cleared her throat. "Cherish, I recall the season you spent those hours down at Lanaeya's. So now I'm guessing Jackson was there with you." Cherish nodded so Madeline continued. "That was a very happy time for you. You hummed in the mornings and giggled at night. You were quite different from the serious child I had always known."

Mr. Baylock sensed Madeline was struggling to arrive at her question. She was cautious not to assign her own emotions from her circumstances to Cherish. They were not the same, and the fact that Cherish was opening up to them was monumental. However, he had spent less time with her trust. Although he wanted to remain on the path to forging their new relationship, he figured he was the person with the least risk to ask the pressing questions. "What your mother's getting at, is given how much you cared for Brandon, it only seemed right to denounce whatever feelings you had for someone else. But did you feel anything for this Jackson?"

Cherish held her breath. Her gums moistened and her palms dried. She released her hand from her mother's. Clutching the cross around her neck, an eleven-year anniversary gift from Brandon, she forced herself to confront the answer. "Love is an obscure son-of-a-gun. The holes it fills are the holes it creates. If feeding a craving is love, then yes, I loved him. Even now in my dreams I sometimes feel the hunger."

19 HIGHS AND LOWS

"I know I can turn you on…Let me touch you where it's
warm

And make it hot…Give you all I've got"

Tierra clumsily tilted her hips from side to side. There was chatter amongst the audience. Once the music stopped, Tierra collected the bills tossed from the few regulars who sprinkled ones on the stage regardless of who was dancing. No one seemed to notice when she had been replaced with the peacock-feathered follow up.

Mr. Cherry was displeased with the lackluster reception of the crowd. As Tierra searched the crowd for whom she'd grant a lap dance to, Mr. Cherry noticed there was an unusually low number of men clamoring for her attention. Her eyes were puffy. Hair was less tamed than he had grown accustomed to. Before she could decide whom she'd waste time with, Mr. Cherry decided he needed to talk with her. He made his way through the crowd. Yanking her into a corner he demanded, "Let me talk to you a second."

Tierra stumbled. "Let go of me. What are you doing?"

Mr. Cherry tried not raising his voice. It was important to him that he didn't upset Tierra too much. His reputation was that of a businessman, but he would not cross the line of pimp. "You're not yourself. You're clumsy and obviously have had way too much to drink. It's not good for business."

Tierra's eyes were nearly shut. Her speech was lazy and even her effort to pull away wasn't much. "I'm just trying to make my money. I'm good."

"No you're not good. You either pack up and go home or go in the back and sleep some of that shit off. Either way I can't let you embarrass this establishment any further tonight."

"Fine. Whatever." She spoke as though she'd take heed. Still, she stood there as if waiting to be dismissed.

"Listen, I don't know and I don't care what kind of family issues or school problems you might have. I don't care if you failed a class or your boyfriend broke up with you. You know why the girls here look happy about what they do? Because they are happy. They recognize that in here they have power over every one of those men and women sitting at their feet. They also have the power to forget their problems at the door and that's what you'll have to master if you think you're going to continue working here. I don't employ victims of life. So get right or get out. You decide what you're going to do."

In a huff, Tierra returned to the dressing room. Bag slung over her shoulder, she made her way into a bathroom stall. *I need some smoke.* She laughed out loud. *He probably thinks because Michelle isn't here I'm all lost on my own. He's just mad because it's thin out there. That's not my fault. It's freaking Christmas Eve.*

Blue sweats and a white sweatshirt made Tierra look as though she was preparing to train as a soccer coach. She leaned against the lever and eased out of the back door. The alley was quiet. Deep breath. *Mr. Cherry is right though. I can't be a victim. This is my life. Everything about it doesn't have to be left to someone else's choosing.*

She walked around to the front. For the first time since she had been at Lucy's, there wasn't a line to get inside. Caden manned the door with frequent scrolls though his cell phone. Tierra took in the air. Cooling her nostrils, it travelled past her voice box and into her chest. The cool clutched the words muddled in her heart. Tears asked to be free, but tonight they'd be denied.

Caden spotted Tierra in the distance. "You done for the night," he yelled.

Tierra nodded. Vigorously her heart leapt, begging to go to him and confide everything that Mr. Leonard had done to her, everything that transpired between her and her grandmother, her and Mr. Cherry. But Caden wasn't equipped to sympathize. No one was.

"Wait a sec! Let me see if I can give you a ride." It didn't matter that she hadn't agreed to stop. He disappeared inside.

Tierra intended to promise him that she'd be fine, although she wondered if she really would be. The frosty air reddened the tip of her nose. She slipped her arms into her bubble jacket. Her fingertips stung with heat despite the plush lining of her leather gloves. So she waited, hoping by some miracle of a chance he'd return with smoke.

Caden was sure not to make any judgment calls when Tierra directed him to the motel she was staying. After pulling into the parking lot he was compelled to ask, "Why are you staying here?"

Tierra's retelling of her lack of credit carried no emotion. "No biggie. Soon I'll be back in the dorm. They reopen after the New Year." Her tone was cold like she had been practicing staying strong.

"I have a credit card."

"So?"

"I'm just saying I could check you in somewhere. Unless you want to stay here."

It was the first time he'd seen her smile for the night. He marveled at how captivating it still was. She was sobering. Her cheeks flushed and he wasn't sure but the oncoming lights made it appear that she wiped away a tear.

"If you're going to be away from your family on Christmas Eve, you might as well be somewhere with room service and premium cable. At least that's what Michelle's mother used to preach."

"You guys are really close. That's nice."

"Most of the women my father dated never made it past the backseat of his Mustang. She stuck around for a few years and was always doing her best to be considerate of me. Honestly I don't know why she and Michelle can't seem to get along. When my dad died she was the only one who wasn't at the repast trying to claim any and everything that wasn't nailed down. But anyway grab your things and I'll get you all set up. This place is definitely not on your level."

Tierra chuckled to herself. *Gran always did say God had a sense of humor. I guess this is my Christmas miracle.* She ran inside and rounded her things then tossing her cases into the back of Caden's SUV. They drove for twenty minutes before he stopped in front of what Tierra thought was prettiest hotel she had ever seen.

White Christmas lights adorned the trees out front. They seemed to light the entire walkway. In awe, Tierra took her time getting to up the hill. Earnestly, Caden took the lead gliding her suitcases behind him. Recognizing the scent of gingerbread and pine, Tierra inhaled, wondering if she'd be able to order up a glass of eggnog. Caden approached the desk, requesting a King suite. Tierra counted out several hundred-dollar bills, but he waved her off.

"Room 407. I think he said the elevators are down this way." Caden handed Tierra the key then settled her luggage onto a baggage cart. "You know when I was a kid I actually wanted to be a bellhop? My dad spent so much time in hotels, conducting business meetings, seeking talent to perform at the club. You know Lucy's used to be a nightclub, right? With singers and everything. The Champagne rooms used to be all one room and be like a lounge setting. So, you had the party folks in one area and the real chill folks in another, but they were all together so to speak. Mr. Cherry is the one who changed it into the Lucy's it is now. I'm sorry, I'm talking too much." He loaded the cart onto the elevator.

Tierra stepped on. She pressed the bubbled 4 then watched as the door closed. *He's so sweet. He's who should've given my virginity to. Maybe he would've taken it easy and it wouldn't have felt like a power drill was cutting through to my damn uterus after.*

Despite the painted gray walls, the white sheets and crimson armchair made the room bright and alluring. Decorative blinking white lights swirled around a five-foot tree against the wall catty-corner to the window. Mints wrapped in green resembled tiny Christmas gifts as they rested on the firm pillows. The sheets appeared clean enough for Tierra to trust there was an absence of bugs, which brought a smile to her face. It seemed the gingerbread had followed them.

Caden settled her bags near the armoire. "Merry Christmas by the way. I see it's after midnight."

Hearing the words, stunned Tierra. Merry Christmas was what she'd whisper in her grandmother's ear every year at midnight. The woman would have fallen asleep on the couch listening to old gospel songs celebrating the birth of the King of Kings. Tierra knew the woman was trying to stay up past the time Tierra would retire. Although she often went up to bed after Madeline, somehow there'd still be a slew of gifts under the tree that weren't there the night before. Her grandmother's voice replayed in her ears, *I'm not going to pretend a man came down our chimney, but we all become Santa when we get in the spirit of giving. Every year you think you've outsmarted me into falling asleep and every year I get a kick out of your face in the morning.*

"Merry Christmas to you too, Caden. Listen, I'm grateful for what you've done here. This room is beautiful. But, I don't want to keep you from your family."

"It's just me in my apartment. I never really did the whole holiday thing. My dad was a traveler, remember?" He gave a halfhearted chuckle.

All the time Tierra had thought about the dysfunction in her own family, it was only now that she was starting to see that he may have had some discord of his own. *When you can only see what's in your head, you shut your eyes to the lives of everyone else. We are not meant to live in this world alone.* Tierra recalled the last sermon she attended. She nodded then proceeded to remove her coat and take his.

As she busied herself getting the coats situated in the closet, Tierra imagined the love that her grandmother poured into laboring over breakfast. The banana pancakes (since she had forever given up her father's preference of blueberry) would send their scent up the staircase and barge their way into Tierra's room for a six o'clock wake up. She'd descend the stairs to find the living room smelling of pinecones and cinnamon candles. Tony Bennett crooning from the stereo speakers would be the soundtrack of their gift giving. Tierra got to pretend that her mother was upstairs asleep in her father's arms. As it had been from the time she could remember, she and her grandmother would have their private gift exchange and bond over hot chocolate and marshmallows.

Tierra wondered if Caden had any traditions he longed for after his father's passing. Talking about it would be too heavy for the first hours of Christmas, she warned herself. *Maybe some other time we can talk of all the things that make our eyes water and our hearts break.* "Excuse me for a moment." She scurried into the bathroom.

Into the eyes looking back at her in the mirror, Tierra peered. Sagging skin hovered above her cheeks. Broken sleep and sobbing mornings were drying her skin. Cooled sweat weakened her edges. She leaned in. Feeling the lump in her pocket, she remembered she had something that would make everything appear beautiful again. Corinne was giving samples out as her Christmas gifts to whoever wanted to partake. Although

Tierra was much past the sampling stage, Corinne had declared she was striving to be without attitude for the holidays. *Lucky us.*

Tierra placed a tablet onto her tongue and washed it back with a palm's scoop of water from the sink. *Oh look, I'm drugging myself. Must've been why Mr. Leonard thought it was okay.* Even she was not amused at her sarcasm. Still after a few moments her mind became less clouded. She could see her reflection through new eyes. Fewer blotches. *I'm nobody's victim. Mr. Leonard didn't do anything but free me. Now that we got the first time out of the way, there's nothing to be afraid of. I do what I want now.* She returned to the bedroom.

Caden stood while he flipped through the channels. Most of the programming disappointed him, yet he searched like he knew there would be something worth seeing. Tierra watched how he carefully steered away from the bed every time he felt himself drift near.

"I thought you were staying a while. Come, sit on the bed."

"Oh my father had a strict rule about people sitting on beds with their 'outside clothes.'" He nodded as if to agree with himself.

"Well, I think we've known each other long enough for me to see you in your boxers. You can take your pants off. You've already seen me naked. Pretty much nightly, I might add."

She had his attention. He gripped the remote and held it to his chest. She wondered what thoughts circled his head as he bit his lip. There was heat tiptoeing up her thighs. She licked her lips. "It's okay. I promise."

Caden sat. Off came his boots. After neatly folding his gray wool slacks and resting them on the dresser, he returned to the bed. However, he remained at the foot. He restarted his search through the channels.

Tierra recalled the confusing tingles she felt when Mr. Leonard was inside of her. She shut her eyes then reopened them, hoping to get his spicy stench clear of her nostrils. She crawled over to Caden and sniffed his neck. "Oh you smell nice. It's a clean scent, but it's more than soap. I like it."

"Thanks." Still flipping.

"You know you can sit back here with me. I don't mind." She wondered about the tingle. Could she feel it without the pain? She read on the Internet that the pain is different when you consent. Most times there's no pain at all. She danced her fingers around his bald head, admiring the dark shine.

"What are you doing, Tierra?"

"Seducing you. Duh. I've seen the way you look at me when I'm on stage."

Caden sighed. He rose and gently pushed her back. Moving too fast for Tierra to process, he reached for his pants then slid his legs inside.

"What did I do wrong? Don't you want me?"

"Tierra, if you think I like you, you're right. However, I'm not stupid enough to think you're fawning over me because you like me. You're high."

"High? I'm not high! I just had a little tiny…" She drummed her fingers across his chest.

He gripped her by the wrist. "You're lonely. I get it. I can keep you company, but I can't sit here and pretend that you being high is the least bit attractive to me."

Embarrassment shifted Tierra's pose and warmed her cheeks. Her thoughts ping ponged with what she imagined his to be.

"You're so damn high and mighty. I'm scum because I work at the same place that pays your bills every week? Leave. Go home to your own lonely and empty apartment. You blew it. You could've had me." She stripped his coat from the hanger.

Caden picked his coat from the floor.. "Obviously, you're having some sort of meltdown, but I'm going to leave just like you asked. Feel free to take the week to steady your head since I paid the room balance until the New Year. Storming out, he paused. "You're welcome, by the way."

Tierra stared at the door after it slammed. Her lungs were filling up with air. Legs feeling as though they would soon give way, she sat on the carpet, resting her head back against the bed. Rejection was a heavy weight that manipulated the ego into the burden of regret. Hugging her knees, she released the anguish that had been flooding her over.

"Why me, she screamed. "Why, God? Why can't I get any peace? Any answers?" Her sobs rippling through her body, she shook and continued to shout, "This isn't fair!"

20 COMING TO TERMS

Jackson Trent was one of the last of the team to walk to the parking lot. A black waist length mink draped over his charcoal suit, he jogged through the wind to his awaiting Chevy Camaro. Winded, he decided that his youthful trot had expired and it was best to brave the cold than to try to beat it.

Through the hazy wind, he spotted his car. To his surprise, he also saw there was a woman leaning on the crimson Cadillac. Clearly struggling to fight the cold herself, she re-wrapped the openings of her wool coat. Despite her fluffy hat, the strands of her hair blew across her chin. Although fruitless, she continued the battle to keep them in place. He'd recognize that serious, "I'm only here for business," stance anywhere.

"Thought they stopped hosting games on Christmas, but I guess not," Cherish called out above the wind. Her smile was slight. She marveled at how much effort it was taking her to appear effortless. *Who knew smiling would be such hard work?*

"This is why I hate when the holiday falls on the weekend," Jackson chuckled.

"Thought I'd get to see you play, but obviously the game's been over."

"Clearly you don't follow football. I've been retired for several years now. No longer the sought after. As a recruiter and analyst, I do the seeking now."

"Oh." Cherish inspected the pavement, searching for something else to say. With Jackson standing beside her, she resolved to state the obvious. "You know I've never been good at small talk."

He leaned toward her. She backed away. Still her floral fragrance seeped through to his being, making itself comfortable. Memories of their entanglement fought to be seen. Her legs spiraled around his. Her supple breasts recalled by his lips. Jackson sighed. This was a much different Cherish. A mother, a widow, and the woman who denied him the right to be a father. Still, with hair blowing across her face, she was breathtaking and his fingers yearned to tug on her curls once again.

"Relax. You're leaning on the driver's door. It's cold. I thought maybe we could sit in the heat."

Embarrassed, Cherish nodded. It was chilly and her old wool coat was yielding to the winds. She felt around in her tattered pocket, hoping she'd find enough tissue to tend to what was sure to be a dripping nose once she spent two seconds in the car heat. Stepping aside, she allowed Jackson entrance then made her way to joining him, in the passenger.

"Of course, it's bewildering to see you here on Christmas. Is everything okay with Tierra? Mrs. Madeline?"

Cherish looked into Jackson's eyes. It was difficult for her to gauge if the calm in her spirit was due to what might be his sincerity or the comfort her eyes recollected when they locked onto his. They still danced as they did when he first introduced himself almost twenty years ago. Just as then, his glare was as though he was blinded by future promises of dreams becoming true. He didn't see the world as it was, but for the possibilities of what his world could become.

Jackson's tone was honest concern, she had concluded. Cherish couldn't call to mind why she felt the need to punish him so. "Tierra walked out on my mother when she came home. Same for Thanksgiving I'm told. Seems she thought returning to school was less dramatic than what was happening at home. Guess I don't really blame her. She's actually not talking to me much, either. Having a hard time processing. But I suppose we all are."

"Understandable."

"Yeah. Do you have any? I mean do you have any others?" Cherish held her breath. Implying Tierra was Jackson's daughter seemed so much easier than saying the words. Although Brandon had already told him about his own impossibility of being Tierra's father, she sensed that Jackson still needed her confirmation. Ignoring the biological facts hadn't kept the confusion far enough under the rug for it not to rise when cleaning house. She couldn't remain upset with Brandon for contacting Jackson. He lived most of his life with decency. If anything, she wondered how many years the want for peace on the subject had taken seat in his mind. Contacting Jackson to make amends allowed him to rest, she was sure.

"No, I never married. I mean not that could technically stop me from having a child, but I guess I never really wanted one without the other."

There was a dense, whispering regret that pushed his words out to her. A child that was his, which he could never raise, and a woman he once had that would never be his were the source of his midnight contemplations. Promiscuous interactions with random women became infrequent over the years. During his career he convinced himself the weightless life of a financially secure bachelor was ideal. However, there were days that he wondered about the beautiful young woman with wild curls and favorable curves. There was light inside of her that he swore only he could reach. He'd call his cousin as a means to be kept in her loop. He found that she too was left with fond memories, but no connection.

"I think in hindsight I desired to have both as well. Somehow in his palm, Brandon held all of my hopes for a family and future. You had a promising career, proof of that in all of which you've accomplished thus far. It would've been foolish of me to assume I could be more than a notch on the promising athlete's belt. We were reckless. And I was scared."

"You wouldn't have been alone."

Cherish turned to face Jackson. "Wouldn't I have, though? Brandon had always intended to marry me. From the beginning he had been my covering, my rock, my safe place."

Jackson's eyes confronted hers. "And what did you view me as? What was I to you?"

Backed down, Cherish lowered her leer to the loose button on her overcoat. She twirled it. "A fantasy."

"If only you knew that you were mine. Being with you was wrong and I can never spew it otherwise. It would be disrespectful to Brandon's memory to attempt. But in your eyes, I saw every dream I was afraid to have. Every time you spoke to me it redesigned my perception of the future. Being next to you made me accepting of my vulnerabilities. Touching you made me feel masculine." His voice was cracking. Holding the emotions down to drown in his blood was becoming overwhelming. He thought of the emptiness he felt whenever his cousin would have no news. Or even more gut wrenching, when she told of Cherish's marriage to Brandon and the suspicion of her pregnancy.

"When you shunned Lanaeya, it hurt her too. The incredible thing is that she understood you felt the need to cut all ties. She helped me understand that it was necessary for the choices you were making." Although he knew Brandon's shoes were not meant for him, he would still imagine himself trying them on. Walking in them for just a day, to be claimed as hers, to share in the joy of expecting a child with her, but as his cousin explained, Cherish was never his. Tainted by each other, yet with her, he felt pure. But he'd have to settle for the prints she left on his heart as all he'd be ever be able to hold of her again.

Cherish blew her nose. The heat was forcing her sinuses into water production and the impending tears only gave it all flow. "This is all very messy and it's my fault. Everything changed for me once the pregnancy came into play. And Brandon…"

Jackson interrupted, "And Brandon was so good. I get it. Listen. I'd tell any other woman in your position that Brandon was the better man. He was kind, consistent, responsible, a great friend even. I was painted as a star with unlimited options. It was expected that I'd take advantage of everything thrown at me. So please rest assured, you did right by yourself by marrying him. Even until the end he remained the better man when he revealed you had almost immediately confided our, our, moment, in him. I intended to tell him, but couldn't bring myself to soil your name, the way it was etched into his soul." He gripped the steering wheel. "Unbeknownst to me, he would be your great sympathizer. Yet, he wasn't so pure to give me the chance to do right by my child during her formidable years. Only when passing could he gift me this revelation. I wonder had he known you'd continue to withhold her from me." His voice trailed off. "A chance to love her; that's all I want."

A bevy of emotions was pouring out of Jackson. It was like someone had removed every barrier that separated the rivers from his valleys. Pulling the spare handkerchief from his coat pocket, he wiped the evidence from his eyes. He had never spoke of his wants to be have a family to anyone save for his cousin, Lanaeya.

Cherish smoothed her coat then unlocked the door. Opening it she swung her feet around to meet the pavement. She sighed, then turned back one last time. "What I came to tell you was that I'm going to work on Tierra coming home for Spring Break. She'll likely be at her grandmother's, if I can get the two of them talking again. I can call you with the dates. Yes, I agree that it's time the two of you get to know each other even if it's the only time she'll allow. You are her father and admittedly, this debt I owe to you."

Resolved in her declaration, she couldn't wait for his reply. Braving head first into the cold, she gave the car door a push. She crossed the parking lot to an awaiting Taxi, choosing to only look ahead.

Jackson watched her as she adjusted her hat for better warmth. Despite the life she kept from him, he wished to envelop her into his chest, offering the warmth she needed. As she entered the back seat of the yellow cab, he mumbled to ears too far away to hear, "It wasn't just Brandon who loved you."

21 WHO ARE YOU?

It had been two weeks since Tierra had last spoken to Caden. What bothered her most was that it had also been two weeks since he had last spoken to her. Neither of them was able to get a handle on the vocabulary that was needed to express apologies, tender feelings, and the glossed over pull between the two of them. Instead, they barely looked at each other, minimally acknowledging one another when in the vicinity. Michelle pestered them both for details, but Caden would shrug in response and Tierra would become irritated.

"Tierra, you're not going to tell me what happened?"

"Michelle, I told you nothing happened. You keep asking me and my answer isn't going to change. Why are you so convinced something happened?"

"Because I know something had to. Every time Caden comes to pick us up to go to work, you decide you're not working."

"Oh, that reminds me, a friend of mine is giving me a lift. I'll probably duck out early."

"A friend? What friend? Wait, don't answer that. No mothering here. But back to Caden. It's pretty obvious you're avoiding him. I asked him about it, but he keeps telling me to ask you. Actually, I'd also like to know how in the devil's nest could anything have time to happen? You went home for Christmas break, although I did hear you worked on the Eve. I don't know how you managed that with your grandmother, the lurker. She must sleep heavy as hell for you to get all the way back here on Christmas Eve. Was the train for you to get back home even running?"

"Michelle, just give it a rest."

"I can't. Since the day you guys met, your face has been lighting up like a casino winning slot machine whenever he's within ten feet of you.

Is it because he doesn't date dancers? Did you try to press him? I told you he has this thing."

"You know what? Yes, Michelle, that's exactly the reason. He doesn't date dancers, so I might as well keep away from him. You've figured it out. Congratulations," Tierra shouted.

"Well, why are you being so secretive about that? Girl, that's understandable. I wouldn't be around someone I liked, but wouldn't date me either. It's a shame cause he does like you. He must. He's mum too, like, won't even reveal that you tried him. Protecting your reputation, I guess. It's sort of chivalrous when you think about it."

Tierra thought back to when Caden slowed his car in front of the hotel with the bright lights. For a second she was able to have hope that he would make her life different. Sadly, she was mistaken. "Yes, shame." Tierra rolled her eyes and strutted off.

Michelle was taken aback by Tierra's bluntness. The cute, warm, unsure Tierra had been tucked away, hidden in the grit somewhere. Whoever she was now had a chip the size of a boulder on her shoulder and venom in her tongue. Michelle stared at the women going to and from the dressing room. *Maybe it's my fault for bringing her here.* At the announcement of Tierra's staged set and the roar of the crowd, Michelle shrugged. *Well she done made it her home now.*

■■■■■■■■■■■■■■■■■■■■■■■■■■■■■■■■■■■■■

At four in the morning Michelle was exhausted. Caden's lack of conversation made the ride seem longer than usual. However, she was thankful that he'd still switch his car for hers so that he could get her breaks changed while she was in class. If she waited for Saturday morning when she was free to take the car herself, the mechanic would charge her an arm and a leg. Fortunately, she had Caden who was the best big brother she almost had. It was too bad that he couldn't confide in her about Tierra. His reluctance didn't stop her from probing though.

"I don't know, Michelle. Tierra seems like she's been drinking like a skid row occupant lately, whispering to Corinne all the time, chumming it up with Raquel. You know what Corinne sells and I don't think I've ever seen Raquel without a joint between her lips."

Michelle snickered. "You sound like an old man. Tierra's not your daughter, my dude. Besides, it's probably nothing to worry about. The girl came to school with a Bible in her suitcase, okay? It's the wild child, freedom for the first time phase. She'll get over it."

Caden nodded. He still hadn't told Michelle about the hotel incident or that he arranged for Tierra to move from the motel. If she knew the conditions Tierra was settling for she would see his point. But Tierra was her friend and he didn't want his opinions to become hers.

"She's been going to class if that means anything to you. That's good, right? Go easy on her. She really likes you and I know you like her.

Otherwise this wouldn't bother you so much. If you want, I'll talk to her and see where her head is. Although, if you're so concerned about her, I don't see why you don't just make her your girl, like official. Get rid of that stupid rule you got or at least make an exception. I've never seen you like this. You guys keep playing this stupid game."

In truth, Michelle was surprised Tierra had been bold enough to give Caden the cold shoulder. He was her one prospect for getting a boyfriend, which seemed to be her goal of freshman year, at least before she started focusing on Lucy's. Maybe she was partly to blame. She shouldn't have spoken for Caden. He didn't typically date dancers, but that was his detail to share. Maybe Tierra got confused with all the time Caden spent talking to her. She should've just stayed out of it. Mixed signals were like mixing brown liquor with white. Whomever drinks it all up will surely regurgitate a mess. Michelle vowed she'd straighten it all out in the morning or afternoon, or whenever she'd be able to think clearly.

The dormitory hallway was dark and silent. As Michelle neared her door, there was the sound of Tierra's laugh. Curious, Michelle cautiously put her key in the door.

Well, I guess she's in a better mood. Maybe we can talk tonight then.

Squeaking open the door, Michelle found Tierra and a familiar gentleman sitting on Tierra's bed. *I hope that's not who I think it is.* The man was a coat of milky caramel. His braids were neat spirals squiggling down his head in six rows. Michelle squinted her eyes. *Damn that's Trig? No wonder she's been shading Caden.*

Comfortably, Tierra's guest sat on the bottom corner of Tierra's bed. Michelle tried to determine how long he'd been there. She cringed at the droplets of melted snow beneath his construction boots. *Been here long enough to drip his dirty ass boots all over the floor. Great!* An extensive, thick gold chain hung over his undershirt. The pendant, which dangled near his stomach, was in the shape of a fist with the middle finger protruding. A black shearling and a man's (she presumed his) beige knitted sweater were thrown onto Tierra's desk. A rhythm and blues playlist resonated from Tierra's laptop. Marijuana fragranced the air, despite the cracked window and the chilled air sneaking in.

Tierra sat poised. Sheer red lingerie adorned her voluptuous curves. She held a marijuana cigar between her fingers. She grinned. The purposeful slamming of the door caused her to jerk.

Through a spell of coughs, Tierra huffed the introductions. "Hey girl! This is Trigger. You seen him before, right? He's been to Lucy's. Trigger, that's my roommate, Michelle."

Trigger nodded. "What's up, Michelle?"

After all Michelle thought she schooled Tierra on, had she forgotten to warn her against inviting a customer to their room? *I'm sure she doesn't know him from a rusty lamppost. Why the hell would she bring him here?* Everyone knew that Corinne sold for Trigger. You'd see him right before Corinne pushed her new batch of work for the week. *Was this the friend Tierra got a ride from? Crap, why didn't I just leave with her?*

There were plenty of times Michelle was intrigued by men offering up a week's worth of shopping sprees just to be allowed to let their fingers linger and their tongues hover. Several times she found herself caught up in the allure of being saved from troubles in exchange for being labeled as girlfriend to a big spender. As a newbie she had done a few deeds to get noticed that she'd now cringe to recall. But quickly she learned there were rules. Albeit unwritten, they were imperative if one wanted to keep safe. She recalled Mr. Cherry's lecture during a rehearsal at Lucy's. *A young dancer, a budding one if you will, must never bring a customer or client back to any place they are living.* She then added, *especially if the space is shared with someone else.*

Michelle kept her head down. She went directly to her side of the room and dropped her bag. She'd have to change in the bathroom. Trigger may have seen much of her bare skin in the past, but this was her abode and she was off the clock. Clearly bothered, she retreated to the hallway.

Offended by Michelle's attitude, Tierra grabbed the half-empty Hypnotic bottle that Trigger drank from. She put her mouth to the spout while eyeing Michelle's side of the room. After guzzling three fourths of the liquid she handed the bottle back to Trigger.

Detecting the tension, Trigger bit his cheek. He watched Tierra's eyes narrow. He could sense the menace in her. Curious to see it mature, he asked, "What's up with your girl? She alright?"

"She's probably just mad I didn't stay to work tonight. You know how it goes when people try to manage you. God forbid you get independent on them."

"She's probably just jealous." He watched for her reaction.

"Oh yeah? That's what you think it is?" Tierra chuckled. "You fine, but you're sure full of yourself. She's good in the man department. I doubt jealousy is what's plaguing her."

Trigger shrugged. "I didn't say she was jealous of you."

Tierra studied his face for a clue. His smirk suggested he was insinuating Michelle had some kind of attraction to her. "You're crazy. And nasty."

"You're right, I'm nasty." He rubbed her thigh and licked his lips. "We don't have to talk about it. Let's just get back to you and I being about it. Michelle is not why I'm here." He dove into her neck while he fondled her breasts.

Pulling away, Tierra stood before him. "You brought it up so let's talk about it. Why would you think she'd be jealous? She's never showed interest in me."

He scoffed. "Look at you with all that fire in your tone." He hopped out of the bed and circled her. Squeezing Tierra's behind, he positioned himself behind her and whispered in her ear. "She did give me top this one time though. So maybe she's not feeling you. Sucks real good," he teased. "But I bet you can do it better." He wiggled his tongue around the rim of her ear.

Tierra squirmed. She likened the sound to a dog lapping water. She guided him toward her breasts. *Does Michelle really go both ways? And what does he mean she gave him top? Maybe he's lying and just mad she rejected him in the past. Although, little Miss Exotic does focus on what I'm doing an awful lot. Hell, she damn near forced Mr. Leonard on me.*

Defiance was rising in Tierra's belly. She had gained the attention of someone Michelle didn't favor or maybe someone who didn't prefer Michelle. But who was Michelle to approve her choices? Tierra swallowed more of the alcohol while Trigger worked his way below her hips. Aware that he was in her pleasure area, she felt the gall to speak up. "That's where you need to be sticking out your tongue."

Trigger grinned. "You nasty too, I see." He proceeded as suggested. In response to her moans he gripped her thighs. His shoulders never caving to her scratches but stiffened under her clasp. He smirked as he slopped. From his pocket he took out a capsule. He paused to open it with his teeth. After spitting the top across the room, he emptied the powdered contents onto his tongue. Without a word, he handed the residues vile to Tierra. He dove back in between her thighs with increased vigor.

Breathing heavily, desperately vying for rhythm, Tierra bit her lip. Prickly tickles strummed her veins and sent her heart racing. Compelled to do something, she sniffed the remnants of the powdered jar. A cold rush surged through her nostrils and rocketed to her head. The already knee buckling sensations below intensified. Speedily she freed herself from the negligee.

"Oh my God, Daddy, that's it right there!" At the onset of Tierra's explosion, she tried shoving Trigger off but he wouldn't let loose until she stopped trembling. When he did rise, she dropped to her knees. Unbuckling his belt, she freed his penis and shoved it into her mouth.

"Tierra!"

Stunned, Tierra's eyes surveyed the room. She furrowed her brow, searching for the culprit. The voice wasn't Michelle's and it was only slightly familiar. She continued to suck, fondled her breasts. Although a bit distracted by the call of her name, she felt the need to swallow him up whole.

Trigger held Tierra's hair while she bobbed. Ecstasy was his highest selling product, partly due to Corinne's diligence in making it available to the women at Lucy's. She told him how loose Tierra seemed to get on the drug. Admittedly, Corinne, too, was turned on when watching Tierra's sensuous high once it took hold at the club. It seemed as though Tierra required little time to reach her peak. It was a no-brainer for Trigger to try her on the powder. With his member currently at the back of her throat, he prided himself on the decision.

Michelle reentered the room. The scene playing before her bulged her eyes and stripped her of composure. "Oh no! This is just too much. If you want to do all of that, you got to go somewhere else. Who does this in a dorm room? Oh heck no!"

Tierra turned to Michelle and grinned. "Why, you want some? I heard you rocked this mic before." She strutted over to her. Despite Michelle's apprehension, Tierra slipped her hand into Michelle's shorts.

Michelle froze. This was not a Tierra she recognized. She had gotten used to the sensuous kitten that took control of the stage at work, but this was something else altogether. It wasn't until Tierra removed her hand, and tasted her fingers that Michelle was able to exhale.

"Feels good, don't it," Tierra flirted.

Recovering from the shock, Michelle shouted. "What are you doing, Tierra?" She backed into the door, securing herself from Tierra's reach.

Tierra rose with fire in her eyes. She drew her fist back and pummeled Michelle's face. Blood spattered the walls. She could feel Trigger scurrying to pull up his jeans. Watching Michelle's nose drip, she scowled.

Michelle cupped her hand over the center of her face. "I can't believe you hit me. You have really gone crazy. I should call the police."

With urgency, Trigger grabbed his sweater and wiped down the bottle of liquor. If there was one place he didn't want to be it was anywhere near a police officer. No sign of him should be left behind. "Calm down. No need to call in the authorities. She's just a little high, that's all. Tierra, get your stuff and come with me. Unless you looking to sleep in a cell, cause I'm not."

Tierra inched close to her roommate. Without warning she issued another blow. She watched as Michelle doubled over, blood continuing to flow from her nose.

Panicked, a fully dressed Trigger added authority to his tone, "On the real, you need to come on. Get your damn stuff and get your ass on out of here, girl!"

Trigger shook his head as he smiled to himself. For months he had been clocking the money Tierra was making at Lucy's. He knew he could make a killing if people paid him for her to dance at his private parties. As a bonus, she got high. He thought, *If someone would have told me long*

ago that pimpin' was this easy, I would have been slinging'
chicks and left the drug game alone.

Still with a daring glare, Tierra dressed
herself in a grey fitted sweat suit. Grabbing
whatever she could from the closet and dresser
drawers, she stuffed it all into her book bag. With
one more look around, she said, "I'm coming
back for the rest of my clothes. You better not
violate either! Go 'head and think I'm playing
with you!"

22 MEMORIES DON'T KEEP TO THE BACK

Another quiet car ride home for Michelle and Caden. After hours of thumping club music, they mutually understood the radio was off limits. The noise would be too much, particularly when they were both struggling to make sense of all that happened. Each with scrambling thoughts, turning over events, questioning how they had gotten to where they were. Angry with Tierra, yet missing her the same.

Michelle scratched at the side of her nose. Appearing as though it had nearly mended, it was still tender from Tierra's attack. As they cruised the highway, she pictured Tierra gripping a bottle of alcohol, funneling the liquid down her throat. *I should've kept her away from Corinne. Or at least warned her. She's doing too much and Corinne doesn't care as long as she makes a buck.*

Caden kept his eyes on the road. It had been a few weeks since he'd seen Tierra. Mr. Cherry asked for her a few nights, but eventually someone else caught his attention. Still, she had Caden's. *What if I would've just let it happen back at the hotel? Maybe she would've have been with that guy. But she was high, I know she was. She might not have remembered and then where would we be? So hard to get a good reading on her. The day we met I should've just asked her out. Or not. Maybe all of this is why I was right to stay away.*

Through his peripheral, Caden eyed Michelle. It was a good thing her nose wasn't broken, although he couldn't say the same for her pride. When she called him to take her to the hospital, it took three washcloths to soak up the blood. In the Emergency Room, she sobbed uncontrollably. She thought of Tierra as a younger cousin. Someone she'd look out for, but give space to live. Even with her mother, Michelle had love, but maintained distance. Tierra had gotten closer to her than he'd seen anyone. He knew that she mourned the loss of a friend more than the sight of her blood.

As they whipped past the women adorning the corners, looking for their night's pay from indiscriminate travelers, clusters of cars with basing music in front of late convenience stores, and stumbling coeds making their way back to the dorms, Michelle recalled when she first met Trigger.

It was her third week at Lucy's. Like Tierra, she was new searching for a new way to assert her freedom. Her parents' divorce became final the day before her tenth birthday. They agreed to remain civil for the sake of their child's backyard celebration. Although what Michelle wished they agreed on, was not to compete with each other over birthday gifts. Her mom threw an over-the-top party equipped with clowns and ponies, and even a band. Not to be outdone, her father made a spectacle, gathering the twenty children in attendance for everyone to see Michelle's brand-new motorized dirt bike. As if she'd be allowed to travel anywhere far alone, it had a GPS and location tracker that linked directly to his cell phone and the local police station. Her mother choked up at the gifting ceremony. However, it wasn't for appreciation of the gesture. It was because her gift of a cell phone and ice-skating lessons seemed to pale in comparison.

When Michelle stumbled across her lust for the exotic stage, she had been to three boarding schools and spent summers in camps on two other continents. One summer she was granted permission to go backpacking across Europe as part of a group tour. She was the only High Schooler in attendance, although that didn't stop any of the post college grads from making visits to her bunker at night.

Although as a freshman she was new to the university, living on her own wasn't unfamiliar. A few friends in her freshman class dared each other to give their inhibitions a freedom pass. Trish, a posh prima donna from Long Island suggested the gentlemen's-club downtown, Lucy's. Flyers were being handed out near the liquor store, promoting the club's Amateur Night. Wasted by the time they arrived, the girls catcalled and laughed during most of the professional performances. Then there was the anticipated call for Amateurs. Only Michelle and one other girl dared to go through with it.

Chucking it up to drunken fun, none of the other girls from the group that night returned to the club. However, Michelle, her interest peaked, came back the next night looking to be taught a few tricks of the trade. Mr. Cherry was eager to get her acclimated.

It wasn't long before Corinne supplied Michelle with samples of everything she sold, anything to rev up her mood to put on an uninhibited show. One night she took Corinne up on her offer to perform at a house party. The allure of not competing with other women for the attention of paying customers was intriguing. Besides, Corinne had assured her that she'd make triple what she made on any given night at Lucy's given the clientele was overzealous when it came to spending money.

An oversized man led Corinne with Michelle following into a walk-up apartment dwelling. Music pulsated through the walls of every floor. Quickly, Michelle surmised at each level there was a party going on. Pop music resonated from the first-floor opened apartment door. As they made their way up the stairs, Reggae sounds could be heard through the hall. Foregoing the third floor and its Techno tunes, the women reached the fourth floor, their destination. There were the remnants of previous sounds, but no open door on this floor. Somewhat impressed, Michelle thought, *Wow! Like a whole V.I.P floor.*

Corinne knocked six times in rapid succession. Someone from behind knocked back. She said her name then added, "And entertainment." What seemed like a shadow opened the door then disappeared.

Fast-paced bounce tunes in both Latin and English flogged Michelle's eardrums. Judging from the shouts of "Aye," and "Bout time," the gathering had been anticipating Corinne's arrival. Alluding to Michelle, she announced that as promised she brought "the goods."

Trigger appeared from a back room with a cigar hanging out the corner of his mouth. A long, thick, gold chain draped around his neck. His pockets bulged and given the respect others in attendance gave him; Michelle pegged him as the organizer and a man she'd like to meet.

"Damn Corinne, she's mad tiny. Don't get me wrong, she's fine as fu…"

Another gentleman interrupted, "Hell yeah she fine. Let her dance for me if you don't want her." He held out a stack of bills. Another man shouted in agreement and the two of them shook hands and waved Michelle over.

"Yeah, she got a little bubble behind her, but where the swollen thighs, the face-suffocating breasts?" Resolving that she would just have to do, Trigger grabbed Michelle by the hand and brought her to the middle of what would otherwise be a living room floor.

Michelle could feel her cheeks redden. Without word she began to bounce to the music. There had never been a man she met that didn't show interest in her. Her thighs may not have been dripping in turkey juice but she knew she could shake, grind, and clap her ass with the best of them. Watching her perform, everyone in the room became exhilarated. The fact that she wasted no time excited most of the party. She used Trigger as a human pole, hand standing against his back and splitting between his legs. Everyone erupted with cheers and applause. The pill Corinne had given her on the ride over kept her energy on ten and her willingness to please was easily interpreted. Her body was on fire and she went an extra mile with every dollar of encouragement. With all attention on her, the women in the room rooted for her the loudest. The more seductively she danced against Trigger, the more money the women showered in.

Completely entranced in what felt like stardom, Michelle unbuckled Trigger's pants and dove in headfirst. He stumbled back, obviously off guard by her gesture. Before the electrified crowd, Michelle bobbed and swirled. Challenged by his inability to become fully erect, she continued while fondling herself, still gyrating her hips and even keeping hold of him while she fell into another split. By the time she was done, she had collected over three thousand dollars. Many of those watching were enticed and offered her additional money for back bedroom private shows. Before Michelle could respond, Corinne declined on her behalf. Amidst pats on her back, Corinne escorted Michelle out and then dropped her off at the dormitory.

The next night Michelle saw Trigger at Lucy's. Believing that she had won him over the night before, she approached him. He gave her a false grin then continued the conversation he was engaged in with a tailored suited gentleman. Michelle tried wrapping her arms around Trigger's neck from behind. She rested her breasts on his back and nibbled his earlobe. Trigger jerked away. He then splashed her face with his glass of whiskey. He shouted, "You don't see I'm having a conversation, Bitch? I told you before that you're not my style. Now go dance for one of them tricks over there. Ain't no money over here for you unless you 'bout to start working for me."

Mr. Cherry rushed over with Caden in tow, ready to force Trigger to leave, but Michelle shook her head and ran off. She ended up in a bathroom stall with her face full of tears and buried in her lap for over an hour. The incident was over a year ago and since then she and Trigger had never made eye contact, until she stormed in on he and Tierra.

Pulling into the dormitory parking space, Michelle looked at all the empty cars. She recalled the night of her incident with Tierra. Trigger shouldn't have been a surprise in her room. She faulted herself for not spotting his car, as the parking lot was usually spotty. *I should've told her who he was, how he was. It was petty of me to keep quiet. Maybe I did still want him to like me.* Michelle hopped out and ran off to her room, letting her tears drip.

23 BOTTOMS UP

"After everything he gives me a damn C," Tierra ranted out loud. Retracing the past few months, she pulled her knees to her chest. The king sized bed she shared with Trigger was covered in textbooks and notepads. She watched the door. Trigger would soon come worry her about her inability to be prompt for any of his parties. She sighed. "One party. I said, one. Now it's a whole damn business. I should of thought of this myself. Michelle would've been down with that."

The mention of Michelle's name brought a flurry of stomach churning visions. It sickened Tierra to recall the way she made Michelle's nose bleed. Rejection had never rested easy with her and Michelle's disgusted protest was unexpected. *Well, I sure foiled that friendship. Love her like a sister and now she probably spits every time she hears my name.*

Tierra shrugged. "It is what it is." She rummaged through the wall length closet.

"Knock, knock." Trigger pushed the bedroom door open. "How did I know you weren't ready? You can't hear the music? People are starting to arrive. They already have a full crowd downstairs." He nestled his beard into Tierra's neck."

"I wish you'd shave that thing. It's so prickly." Holding out a two-piece thong set with fur around the edges and a revealing zebra print leotard, she pulled away then turned to him.

Trigger pointed to the leotard. "Can't give it all away at once mama." He sat at the edge of the bed. "Did you shower yet?"

Tierra ignored the question. It was obvious from the dry towel and washcloth she had just pulled from the top of the closet that she hadn't gotten to it. Verbalizing it didn't seem like it would help matters. Trigger was cool most of the time, but whenever she admitted to falling short on a task or promise, he'd get explosive. If she said she'd cook, but didn't, he'd yell expletives even while she reluctantly readied the pots and pans. If she forgot to clean the stove afterward, he'd have another conniption. If it weren't for the free pills and endless supply of smoke, she'd die of migraines from listening to all of his tantrums.

As she headed to the bathroom, Trigger grabbed Tierra's elbow. "So we on some new stuff? When I speak, you don't answer me?"

"C'mon, I'm trying to get ready. You know I didn't bathe yet. I'm heading to the shower. You see my stuff in my hand. Don't kill the mood before I go out there, okay? I'm already bummed since I finally had a look at last semester's final grades."

Trigger nodded. "You get a pass this time cause we got some money to make. Don't make it a habit."

Hoping to settle the beast she could see looming behind his eyes, she kissed his cheek. He grinned then tightened his grip. This time she remained quiet. Saying too much had never worked out for her in the past. She felt this was a time when her silence would be appreciated.

Trigger dug in his pocket. He took out a sandwich bag full of pills. He put one in Tierra's palm. "I'm sorry. Don't let me blow your mood. By the time you finish showering you should be good." He stood. When he kissed her lips he pressed.

Tierra glanced at the bag. Trigger was placing it back in his back pocket. Although thankful for the means to get her head in the game, she wished he would've given her more than one. Tonight, it'd take twice as much to stop asking herself why the hell was she still there. She'd need the whole bag to ignore what she knew to be her father's disapproval, gnawing at her conscious. *Well, Dad, guess you shouldn't have left me…* She shrugged as she placed her hand beneath the faucet, feeling for its temperature.

24 GOODBYES DON'T HAPPEN AT FUNERALS

"Lay all your troubles… At his feet…" The soloist belted the tune as many of the mourners nodded. An elderly woman, her face hidden beneath a black veil, seated in the back row of the parlor waved her hand into the air, screaming out, "Yes, Lord!" God's reverence had sounded unfamiliar to the woman's tongue, according to Tierra's ear. But then she recalled her father's pleas to not put too much stock in his grandmother, her great. Instead she tried focusing on the top-heavy woman's whose veins pulsed as she belted.

First the wake, then the service. It was agreed that one day of viewing was best, for Tierra's sake. No one wanted to subject the twelve-year-old to her father's stiff, made up and stuffed body more than once. If only her mother was as mindful when arguing with the director over why her husband's skin was made to look like blushed clay. And made less of a fuss over the wrinkles in his suit.

Who agreed to spare the girl? Tierra wasn't sure, particularly since they hadn't stopped anyone from adding his picture to the obituary section of the newspaper. The one classmate who had her number called to offer condolences and then promptly notified what seemed like the entire school of her father's passing. Assuming she was grieved, she was excused from classes, gym, and left out of conversations.

Whomever this mysterious, inconsistent decision maker was (her mother was much too distraught to even feed her let alone decide what was best), had miscalculated her devotion to the man who held her hand on the first days of school. The man who talked her down from the tree branch when she had climbed too high; rocked her to sleep on nights when the striking sounds of thunder caused her legs to shake. She'd continue to return a hundred more days if it meant that she would have the chance to declare her love to her father again. She worked to convince everyone that she was okay, wiping her face dry whenever entering the parlor, managing a subtle smile. She'd offer to collect the sympathy cards and arrange the flowers, stomping her feet whenever dismissed from the company of tears. But it was like she herself was a ghost. No one could hear her protest through the noise of the dark. They'd mutter about what she might be feeling as though she was off playing in the woods and not right there, present and listening. Often, late at night she contemplated the possibility that it was true; she was just a spirit, fantasizing a life that had long passed. Maybe alongside of her father, she died too.

Under the dim lights and too close to the microphone, the preacher spoke of Brandon Proper, "A great man," he knew of, but was never so blessed to meet. The organist swayed as he played. The soloist sang a hymn selection. Onlookers chanted, "Amen," and hollered shapeless sounds of their sorrows. Tierra turned to see that her great-grandmother was no longer in attendance.

Crying women with oversized hats fanned away the heat of busy emotions despite February winds gusting against the window pane. Cherish remained still, rigid, resigned to not lending her voice to the chorus of sobs.

The women, many of them nurses who worked at the hospice with her father; who were then required to tend to him during his last days, rocked back and forth. Their moans dragged on. Like a game of double-dutch, each one seemed to have waited her turn to jump in so no bellows went unheard. The men patted their foreheads with white handkerchiefs, overwhelmed by the number of hugs they had to give and the hands that needed to be respectfully shaken.

Cherish remained. Tierra wondered if maybe her mother found a way to communicate with her father's spirit. The way she stared at the casket was like she was telepathically conversing with the man whose arms she had lived in for the past thirteen years. Or perhaps she had found a way to endure the pain of missing him. A superpower Tierra had yet to possess.

Tierra tried sitting still. Her chair was sandwiched between her mother's and grandmother, Madeline, in the front row of the room, a close enough view to where her father rested. She worked through the probability of escaping into the realm of her father's spirit. If she could close her eyes and concentrate, the scent of the accumulated flowers would fade. Voices would silence. She'd feel as though she was floating, but it would only be her spirit going to meet her father's. *Brandon. Brandon? Brandon.* Nothing. *Daddy. Daddy? Daddy.* Still nothing. *Maybe he won't speak to me because I'm so easy to see.*

Everyone would know he's here and his presence is probably supposed to be kept a secret. At five foot seven inches, Tierra sat as tall and, in some cases, taller than other mourners. If only she could conjure some sort of wind where'd she be able to detect his voice in the whistle. She could find some way to prove to him that if he came to her she would keep his secret. After several more tries of focusing on his name, calling upon the power of the wind, she opened her eyes. The odds had declined her favor. She was destined not to enter any universe outside of the one that left her without her father.

Tierra's palms moistened. Her knees bounced. Even with the towering, wide fans spinning at maximum speed in each corner of the room, the air felt stale and insufficient. Sweat sprinkled her forehead. Despite her dress being sleeveless she felt imprisoned by the chiffon clinging to her skin. The room was becoming blurry. Faces morphed into what looked to be melting plastic and her tongue was suddenly dry. Frantically, swiveled. Distorted heads were all buried in prayer. The room was silent although mouths opened and hands still slapped laps or shot up in testimony.

Tierra felt herself gliding although she remained seated. All sound was muting. There was no breathy sobbing and the soloist's serenade had been reduced to a mouthed interpretation.

She rose from her seat and headed toward the back. The room was small, but as Tierra quickened through, the water fountain in the room's distant corner appeared to continue to remain as far as when she first saw it. Her mouth dry as desert sand, she was forced to swallow the salted speckles of saliva. She opened her mouth hoping to breath in something that would wet her palate, but it was just more air. Imagining her tongue disintegrating into dust, she inhaled deeper, exhaled faster. She would need to run at top speed to make it to the fountain. Her knees were heavy, but she found the strength to get them forward.

Once within arm's reach of the silver quencher, the sniffles and loud cries suddenly returned to the room. Mr. Baylock grabbed Tierra, enclosing her into his arms. She struggled to pull away. Against her face, Mr. Baylock's black suit jacket became like the folded paper towel of chloroform in the murder mystery shows Tierra had as of late become addicted to. Much like the kidnappers' intentions, she feared Mr. Baylock was using it to lull her to sleep. The more she tried pulling away, the tighter he squeezed. Her head was dizzying. *Oh God! Is this what I asked for? Am I going to die?* Convinced her demise had been near, the few tears she was finally able to cry, rolled down her face. Quickly her heart began to lighten with the joy of promise as she thought that in death she might be reunited with her father. She grinned. Within seconds, Tierra gave into her collapse. Everything went black.

25 TAKE COVER

"Tierra, it's your mother. Call me."

"It's Gran, baby, call me. You know I've never gone this long without speaking to you. I've tried to give you your space, but you're still my baby. We can work this all out. Call me."

"Tierra Genelle Proper! Enough of this not speaking to your grandmother. Me, I can understand. I know you're hurting and confused, but don't act like your grandmother hasn't treated you like gold all your damn life. So, we've got secrets. By now, I'm sure you have a few of your own. It's time we all woman-up. I'm not going to stop calling so you might as well call one of us."

"Honey, I called your room and your roommate said you weren't staying there? I didn't want to pressure the young woman but she did say you guys had some sort of fallout. Tierra, call me. Where are you staying? Michelle, I think she said that was her name. She said you weren't out on the street, but then Tierra, where are you? You're not answering is making me worried. The young woman was

kind enough to assure me that she saw you frequently. At least you're alive, but honey, you can always come home if it's not working out for you out there."

Concentrating on her research assignment for which Tierra had to write a three-minute speech was feeling insurmountable. Had she not been lost in the tunnel of her family soap opera, trying to forget the altercation with Michelle, and disillusioning herself about no longer feeling anything for Caden, she would have remembered her grades were dependent on doing actual work.

Nightmares of the night Mr. Leonard robbed her of her virtue gave her heart palpitations. Her mind would reason that she had her womanhood dangling for anyone to grab, but in the pit of her stomach there was a red-faced, seething beast kindling her rage. Every detail snuck its face behind corners, shadowed behind faces throwing dollar bills, causing her to sometimes flinch when one of Trigger's clients slid their fingers in the sides of her G-string.

Then he rated her a C. Tierra shook her head. "Maybe I earned a C in Statistics. I sure enough wasn't bright enough to not become one." Tierra fell back onto the bed and kicked at the air. She screamed to the ceiling fan, "I hate him, I hate him, I hate him!"

Tierra!

She was quiet. Certain she was alone in the room she shook her head and continued to talk to herself. *Am I in the damn Twilight Zone? These folks right here bout to drive me crazy.* She opened the walk-in closet to be sure no one was hiding. *I mean who would be stupid enough to hide in Trigger's closet. It's not like he'd be playing that game. His ole non-playful ass.* She grabbed the baseball bat hidden behind the bed. Other than rows of hung clothes and the display of Trigger's over organized (her repeated opinion) racks of sneakers and boots, the closet was empty. *This is some next level paranoia mess. It has got to be from all those crime shows I watched at Gran's cause I haven't seen TV or a movie in three lifetimes.*

Again, the voice echoed her name. Pinpointing the voice was difficult. She was sure she never heard it before, yet it felt familiar. Maybe similar to her father's she thought, but younger. It was foolish. She had only known his voice to sound one way; well, other than the weak version that whispered from his hospice bed. Thinking back to the stories her father told of puberty with knobby knees and voice changes, Tierra realized what she heard was what she imagined his voice to be like before the first change. Brandon was always so vivid with his recounts of childhood; she'd swear she heard every sound he described. This voice that was calling her name, it was young, as a maturing boy who had just attained his baritone. However, she reasoned it was impossible for the voice to be any realer than when her father told of it. She went into the kitchen where Trigger was making himself a sandwich.

"Did you call me?"

Trigger shook his head and went on to spread the mayonnaise on the whole grain bread. Meticulously, he laid the turkey slices across, then two slices of provolone cheese. Although he could feel her watching, he wouldn't look up. Carefully he sliced a tomato on the wood cutting board. Still holding the knife, he finally turned to her. "T-Bags, you better lay off that smack if it got you hearing shit."

"I hate when you call me that. It's like you're talking to someone else or to your nuts or something. Anyway, I thought I heard you say my name. But my name was said correctly, so I guess it wasn't you."

Exasperated, he rested his sandwich on the wood. He pushed his fingertips into the edges of the kitchen island. "Didn't I say, no? I don't know what's with you and your name. In your sleep, you ask who's calling you. Every time the room is too quiet, you looking around like you heard something. I don't need you going crazy.

We got a party tomorrow night. Don't be all asking my guests who said your name and how they know it, and all that girly foolishness y'all chicks do. I'm trying to build a business. This is not Lucy's. I'm the only one up in here that's allowed to be crazy," he sneered. He then loaded his sandwich into the toaster oven.

Tierra retreated to the bedroom. No one ever told her she talked in her sleep. She recalled the nights when she and her grandmother would spend the night with Cherish. Although Cherish had been of few words, she'd ramble in her sleep apologies and declarations of love to who Tierra assumed was her father. *Damn you, Cherish. You better not have passed on your loony antics to me. Well, I can't really have her crazy. She wasn't talking enough. Seem like my head is talking too much. Geez, I sound like Gran now.*

Refusing to say it aloud didn't change the longing she felt. Tierra missed her grandmother. *How could I have missed Christmas? That was really selfish of me. But it's her own fault for trying to force Jackson on me. I don't hate her. Even love Mommy with her complicated ass. They know that. I'm not ready to call, though. Just need to breathe. Once we stack some money and I help Trigger open his club, I'll have my own money for my own education (if I even need school at that point). Jackson is probably just throwing money on the table to buy his way in. If the ball players who've come in to Lucy's are any indication, that's what men like him do. Gran is old so she doesn't know. She's thinking about securing my future. It's not wrong because honestly, I've thought about it, but I don't need him.*

Sadness weighted her shoulders. Michelle had once asked her why she despised Jackson so much. It was a difficult question to answer, as she never asked it of herself. Maybe it was the ease of everyone to use him to replace Brandon. Accepting Jackson would mean that Brandon had a flaw. A man who'd pretend that the father of the daughter he was raising didn't exist unbeknownst to the father himself, seemed vengeful; not a characteristic Brandon would ever be described as. It wasn't that she didn't empathize with the struggling for clarity, but she couldn't do it at the expense of the man who'd let her sip his coffee and made the best blueberry pancakes on Saturday mornings.

Tierra's eyelids twitched. Contemplating the reality of what was worse, the work she had to put in to avoiding tears or how often she had to fight them. *I hate feeling like this. My dad was a good man. I know he was!* She peeked out around the corner of the bedroom. Trigger could be heard arranging to meet one of his handlers later that night. He muted the television, which allowed her to listen for his footsteps. There were none, but she could hear the remote clamoring onto the coffee table. She pictured him pacing the carpet.

Quietly, Tierra slipped into the closet. Amazed at the ease in which she was able to move about without his scrutiny, she tiptoed back over to the bedroom door, re-checking for any sign of him. He had made another call. This time his voice sounded less aggressive. If she didn't know better she'd think he was whispering. Still, she needed something to quiet it all together.

Back over in the closet, Tierra rummaged through every one of Trigger's pockets until she found what she was looking for. She knew Trigger would sometimes drop a few pills in his pocket when he neglected to close the zip lock bag all the way. She likened the occurrences to when her french-fries would fall out into the bag. After finishing them it would feel like she was gifted bonus gold when she'd dig through the bag before trashing it.

Within three days she had run out of the two-week supply of Ecstasy Trigger had given her as well as the stash she had in her bag from Corinne. Asking for more would just be inviting more of Trigger's judgments, which he happily shared. On several occasions, he insinuated that she might have a problem. Confidently she'd offer her rebuttal, "I'm not dependent. I have a lot going on in my head and this helps me feel good. When my ass is up in the air or when I'm slopping you down, you don't think the pills are a problem then. Besides, seems like your whole customer base likes my performances when I feel good." She'd smirk and lick the side of his face. The conversations usually concluded with her hoisting her ankles while he conceded with thrusts.

Tierra kept the two pills she was able to find concealed in her hand. She casually strolled into the kitchen. First, she ran the sink faucet to see if the sound would lure Trigger in. He remained on the phone. Although, the hush in his voice disturbed her, Tierra scolded herself. *Look, it's either he's minding your business, or you minding his. Which is it right now?* She decided to take her glass of water back to the room. Downing the E in the center of the kitchen was too risky with Trigger in the next room. If the pill could calm the voices in her head, she might be able to get through writing her speech, or at the very least be able to take a nap. The past few weeks had felt as though sleep was only an occasional visitor.

After half an hour, Tierra was feeling lightheaded. The room was blurry. Drapes distorted, the carpet looked like furry monsters grabbing at her feet, and the walls seemed to close in, then back out. Then, a sense of peace washed over her, followed by a gust of angst, and then a calming heat. The mahogany wood of the headboard and nightstands were suddenly reeking of polish. The sea blue down comforter looked like a relaxing ocean wave.

So, Mr. Leonard is a jerk. Tierra chuckled. *Okay he's more like a jerk-off. And now this dude, Trigger parading around here like he's the man. Neither one of them worth the shits they take. I know that's a bitch he out there love-jonesing on the phone with. Bet you he'll get off that phone if I go in there and sit on his face.*

Tierra entered the boxed living room wearing one of Trigger's zip-up hooded sweatshirts. She stood in front of the television, authoritatively posed in red pumps, zipper pulled down to mid-cleavage, and hands on her hips. Due to the fact Tierra was two inches taller than Trigger, and he wasn't the beefiest of guys, the sweater snuggled her curves and barely covered the top of her thighs. Her hips bulged at the sides.

Trigger, mid cigar-roll, looked up to find Tierra's red glossy lips demanding to be noticed. "Um, I'm going to call you later. Never mind why. Just hang the damn phone up." He placed the phone on the glass coffee table. His eyes still focused on the long-legged siren before him, he licked the rolled cigar then burned its tip with a lighter.

As Trigger inhaled then blew his first puff, Tierra strutted over to him. She straddled his thighs. Capturing his bottom lip with her teeth, she took his free hand and rested it on her bottom.

Trigger locked eyes with Tierra. He squinted. When she smiled, her eyes half closed, he broke free of their embrace. Suddenly hostile, he shoved Tierra. He watched as she stumbled back. "You high?"

Ignoring his question, Tierra pounced again. Despite Trigger squirming and holding her arm's back, she pushed, trying to will herself forward.

"Girl, you better look at me! Are you high?"

Her body feeling weightless and her insides thirsting to be touched, Tierra huffed and replied, "Yeah, I'm high. What's your point? I'm trying to get you high if you let me," she giggled.

"So what? You a goddamn addict! You think I don't know you finished all them drops that I gave you? I'm supposed to be hard-pressed for your big, junkie, ass?"

Tierra scoffed. "Junkie? You're bugging. Come on babes. Let's not fight." She bit the tip of her finger. "I'm feeling a little empty. Just give me a little something to fill me up." She patted her thigh.

"What you on, that E? Where'd you get it? Stole it?" He tucked his bottom lip. "So, you think that I'm a fool who can't count. You think I don't realize my supply be light every night. Like I don't leave them damn pills behind to test you. You must be out your rabbit-ass mind!"

Sheepishly grinning, Tierra rebutted, "I might be. But you know what they say about sex with a crazy chick…"

Whap! Trigger backhanded her face. "Ain't no pennies for your thoughts. I'm talking about a loss of money and you declaring to be a damn cliché."

Tierra's head vibrated. She held her cheek. It stung. *Did this bastard just slap me?* The swelling was quick to begin. Her jaw was starting to tighten.

They both contemplated what was next. Trigger anticipated having to strike her again. Tierra was deciding how she would defend herself before he concluded her as someone to go down easy.

As if a match bell rang, Tierra leapt toward Trigger, her fist balled. She swung, but he blocked. Then he captured her other looming fist. She struggled to break free.

Trigger spun Tierra around. He cinched her neck in his forearm and forced her into his chest. "Bitch, I don't know who you thought I was, but I'm not him."

Leaned back against his stomach, Tierra could feel the grip of the pistol he kept tucked in his waistband. She made a plan to grab it. She'd point it at him, and then hold him at bay until she could make it out of the apartment. If she could get her speeding heart to slow, she'd be able to get her hands to stop trembling.

An elbow to his gut didn't land with the power Tierra intended. Although she was bigger than Trigger in both height and girth, she was no match for his strength. Desperate to be free, she chomped down onto his hand, refusing to let go even after the skin was broken.

Livid at the sting of his own blood, Trigger shoved Tierra. The force compelled her to fall to the ground. Bing! Her forehead hit the metal sofa post.

Tierra's ears rang. She could feel her head opening up. The room was spinning. She gripped the carpet for support. On all fours, she crawled towards the door.

Unfinished, Trigger hovered over Tierra, his hands reaching for her hair. His gold chain swung between her face and his tummy. One hand gripped securely around her loosening bun, he then grabbed her chin, squeezing with all his might.

Tierra's mind was racing. *Is he going to kill me? I think he's going to kill me. I swear God, if you let me out of this, as soon as he goes to sleep tonight, I 'm getting out of here. But not before I burn his ass with some hot chicken gristle.* A fisted blow to her temple jumbled her thoughts.

"That school ain't teaching you nothing, I see." Trigger issued another punch to Tierra's head. "Today though, you're going to learn who the hell I am." Forcing his way around her flailing arms, he gripped her wrists then punched her in the mouth. "You think it's okay to steal from me? Then you gonna bite me like you some damn rabid animal? And you've been running around here with your smart-ass mouth like it's all cool." Re-gripping her hair, he hauled her to the middle of the floor. "I ain't one of those chumps from that stupid club nor am I your boy, Cherry. You think that toy security guard gonna come save you? How many times I gotta tell you that I'm running this here?" He threw another exclaiming jab to her jaw.

Broken gums and shaky teeth, Tierra's blood poured. Images of Mr. Leonard atop of her flooded in. The pungent odor of sweat and stale breaths circled her nostrils. Flashes of Michelle's leaking nose and eyes full of shock and horror interjected. Powerless against the current feet attacking her ribs, Tierra was overcome and afraid that she was going to suffer her death, leaving no one to mourn. No one outside of her grandmother ever put hands to her face, much less the knee to her throat Trigger was pressuring.

Trigger taunted, "I thought you were about this life! You want to beat up on your little old roommate who's half your size, though. Get up! You can do more than bite right? Or you're only good for using your mouth? Fight back!"

Tierra was winded. Catching her breath only yielded to coughing when it didn't escape her too quickly to fill her lungs. If she could only scream loud enough for someone, her grandmother, her mother, Caden, or even Michelle to sense she needed help. The building was filled with those who either attended a Trigger party or copped their vice from him. Who would come to her rescue? The voice that constantly repeated her name told her to shout anyway.

"Help! Help!" Alas, her screams went unanswered. Her eyes watered. That voice wasn't real unlike the slicing pain in her abdomen. Drops of teary salt burned her lips. A sound likened to a television emergency signal test pulsed through her eardrums. She tried to shield herself, but the pain only stopped when her body went numb.

With Trigger breathing heavily, Tierra sensed the onslaught might soon be over. If she could just close her eyes and rest, maybe she'd wake up and this would all be a drug-induced nightmare. She felt her head being snatched up then slammed to the floor. The under-shoe grit of gravel and mud mixed with her saliva and blood. The tainted lint forced its way onto her tongue. Finally, Tierra could feel Trigger shuffling away from her. Still her eyes were too heavy to open. She felt the weight of a towel tossed over her.

"Clean yourself up. I bet your ass is sober now." Trigger chuckled. He revisited the ashtray that held his rolled cigar. He grumbled, "Now look at me! All sweaty and what not. When I get out of the shower you better be in that bedroom with your ass high and head low too. Since you want to give it out so damn bad."

Tierra listened for the running water. Weak and achy, she crept up. Opening her eyes proved difficult with one lid growing plump. Bruises on her face bloomed beneath her fingers. Limping, she made it to the coat closet. Gingerly she pulled her gym bag from the corner. Relieved she found a pair of leggings balled up. Too scared to take the time to dress in them she placed them back in the bag. Reaching for the heaviest coat she owned, she draped herself in it. She then slid her feet into a pair of gold tennis shoes she kept for quick store runs.

Tierra grabbed the doorknob and removed the chain. She could hear that the shower water was slowing. She paused. Trigger was humming as he typically did when drying off. Swiftly, Tierra opened the door, let herself out, and then took off running down the six flights of stairs to the lobby. Somehow, she was graced with a second wind which allowed her to pick up pace. The weight of her duffel reminded her she never took her cell phone out from the previous night. The thought encouraged her steps, fueling her to take flight. She ran out of the dwelling doors, gaining speed with each stride. She'd run all the way to her mother if she had to.

26 I'D FIGHT FOR YOU

Caden pulled into his regular spot in Lucy's parking lot. Patrons were already lined around the corner. *I guess we have a few guests in town. Geez, I hope I won't have to throw out any singers tonight. They always want to sue for something they started.*

Mr. Cherry hadn't forewarned him of the possible large turnout. Finding it odd, he glanced down at his phone. Two missed calls. *Michelle must've been trying to warn me.* He scrolled to the next number. *I'll have to call Tierra back tomorrow when I have the time.* He sighed. *This whole thing with her and Michelle is crazy. I really thought one day she'd my girl.* He chuckled at his naïveté.

With Tierra's absence from the club, Caden's thoughts would often drift, trying to imagine what she was doing. Then he'd immediately shake it off as Trigger's face would pop into his head, forcing him to recall that's who she chose to be with. There was something going on with her, but he couldn't quite get a hold of what it was that had her so offbeat. She was definitely different. He assumed it was all the different pills and alcohol Corinne was pouring into her, but there had to be something else, a marked change. Looking back at her missed call, he promised himself he'd call her soon as his shift was over.

"Caden, I'm glad you're here." Mr. Cherry ushered Caden through the door. "Charles has the door for right now. You, I need inside tonight." His arm around Caden's shoulder, Mr. Cherry bent Caden for his ear. "You're my go-to guy, you know. We've got a wild mix in here tonight and I got a strange feeling about it all. I just need you to be on point."

Surveying the great room, Caden agreed with Mr. Cherry's assessment of the crowd. Of course, there were the usual gawkers who never left the rim of the stage. Peripherally, he spotted the heavy drinkers that took up residence at the bar every night. However, he counted at least four groups of sash and glitter-adorned women celebrating upcoming nuptials. Another clique was screaming "hallelujahs" over a recently decreed divorce (as announced on one of the women's t-shirt). Over by the photo wall were some local musicians, posing for pictures with several of the dancers. A few pockets of fraternities and sororities in their branded gear sat opposite the leveled booth that held fledgling football players and recruiters. Sprinkled about were the rolled-up sleeves of "businessmen" with "Out of Towners" resonating from their auras.

Still with thoughts of Tierra weighing heavy on his mind, Caden nodded. He caught a glimpse of Corinne bringing drinks back to the dressing room. *If Tierra could've avoided contact with Corinne, she and Michelle might've still been friends.* Over the past two years he had seen Corinne service many of the women without a care for how they would handle whatever she was pushing. Some of the girls had never touched anything more than marijuana before. However, after meeting Corinne many of them had tried every drug available in the city. All she wanted was her pockets lined.

"Mr. Cherry I got you. However, I do need to talk to you about Corinne."

Caden tried to be patient. He perceived Mr. Cherry's rapid speech and constant checking over his shoulder as nervous energy. He got that way when the money barometer threatened to go off the meter.

"I hear you, Caden. For now I just need you to check on the girls in the back. We got a lot going on and my trust is in you." He shoveled Caden along.

After making it halfway to the dressing room, Caden decided to stand his ground. "No, Mr. Cherry this is important. Corinne is selling again and I know you know she is. The girls are getting hooked and it's out of control. In particular…"

Mr. Cherry nodded quickly. "Yeah, yeah, I know Tierra." He stopped and looked Caden in the eye. "I pay attention to everything. Tierra's behavior and constant interaction with Corinne was obvious. Then she just drops off the scene? Corinne didn't bat an eye at her new friend's absence. That low level hustler, Trigger hasn't given me any hell lately either. Hardly see him. Doesn't take a brain surgeon." He looked out into the busy bustle of the night. "Police should be by soon to pick up Corinne. I can't have you and Michelle going round here all crazy like with your friend gone. You liked her and I know you worry. I'll let you know when they get here. Now do you trust that I'm way ahead of you on this?"

Caden grinned. He patted Mr. Cherry's shoulder. "You're alright. You haven't changed."

"Damn right I haven't. And that's on your father's grave. Now please get to the back. I don't need pandemonium to break out when the damn police get here. We've all got jobs to do. Money don't stop just cause she's getting knocked."

Caden agreed and walked the remainder of the hall. He passed by the section that was typically roped off for visiting celebrities. Overhearing a conversation that mentioned Tierra's name gave him pause.

"My daughter, Tierra goes to your school. Do you know her? Before I entertain you as a viable candidate for the draft I'm going to want to know the answer to that." Jackson Trent was chuckling and eyeing the player for response.

Just then a dancer scurried from the back. She held a robe to her breasts. Relieved to see Caden she grabbed his arm. "Come quick. That dude, Trigger's back there looking for Tierra. He's high on that white or something. Got his gun out talking about we hiding her."

Caden followed the woman to the dressing room. As they got closer the passageway became cramped with dancers arguing with whom Caden assessed to be members of Trigger's crew. They were trying to gain access to the back.

Meg, a redhead, tattooed performer who only worked the tables, loudly exclaimed, "Selling drugs and being about these hands ain't the same thing. Don't get cut!" She challenged any man willing to oppose.

As Caden pushed his way through, he spotted Noodle shoving a gentleman who was trying to bulldoze his way past her. Caden yanked several onlookers aside, "Security coming through. Security."

The crowd was hard to order. A veteran dancer, Veronica, got tired of holding the men off. With balled fist and precise aim, she long swung; forcing a young bald man with gold for teeth, to fall back, nursing his eye.

"Oh, bitches swinging? It's on now?" The young man jumped back toward Veronica, unable to connect. There were a swelling number of women blocking the entrance. A bigger acquaintance, adorned in three gold chains, joined the fight by grabbing one of the women by the neck. However, his antics were met with several women sideliners now willing to be engaged in what was quickly morphing into a brawl.

Caden squeezed through an array of swinging fists. He pulled women from pounding the tops of men's heads. Making use of the emergency exit, each man he freed, he tossed outside. Women, he worked to decipher if they were Lucy's employees or drunken patrons with no real investment in all the action. The dancers, Caden commanded either out of the door or onto the floor to work.

Finally, at the entrance of the dressing room, Caden located Trigger. Atop a stool, the local dealer folded his arms, although gripping his gun. The women, who feared making a move, remained his audience. Once again, he announced

he'd make himself comfortable until someone
gave up Tierra's whereabouts.

"Tierra Proper?"

Jackson Trent came from behind Caden.
The melee forced him to protect his prospects.
After securing their safety, he was compelled to
assist Caden in making it through the commotion.
For each thug Caden casted out, Jackson subdued
the faction surrounding. Through the punches
and shouts he heard very little of what started the
riot, except the name, Tierra. He had not spotted
her during his visit nor did he expect her name to
be on the tongues of anyone in a place such as
Lucy's.

Trigger smirked, "Why yes, Old Man. Are
you her new Sugar Daddy or something? Cause
she still owes me some bread." He smiled broadly
while twirling his gun.

"What is it you think she owes you for?"
Cautiously, Jackson stepped closer to the gunman.
He considered the few hundred he had in his

pocket. *I can't imagine it would take much to pay this imbecile to settle his grievance.*

Caden tugged at Jackson's arm. Mr. Cherry would have a fit if he allowed this legendary player to get hurt in his club. Jackson allowed the pause. However, Caden could feel the man's limb stiffen. It was hard as an oak tree trunk. He was preparing to fight. *If Trigger isn't careful, he'll have to meet this man as his overcomer. Nothing but the bullets in that gun would save him.* Still it was Caden's place to do his best to keep all customers safe. Decidedly, he spoke up. "Gordon, look we don't want any trouble. Tierra's not here. Hasn't been here."

Nostrils flared and muscles flexed, Trigger turned to Caden. "Did you just call me… Trigger, boy, that's who I am! You want me to show you why?" He stormed over to match Caden's glare.

Nose to nose, Trigger grilled Caden, pointing his gun up at his chin. Caden remained solid. He stared into Trigger's eyes. Then from the left came a thick-fingered fist that knocked Trigger to the ground forcing him to lose grip on his gun. The gun spun out onto the floor setting off a random shot. Women screamed. They rushed the door as Caden and Jackson followed in Trigger's dive for the gun.

27 CHASING FREEDOM

Tierra had lost count of the blocks she ran. Repetitiously, visions of gracing the stage at Lucy's came to mind. She moved. The lights provided sauna-like heat beaming down on her shoulders. She glided. Sprinkled with loose bills, the stage yielded to her every step. He slid his money to her on the side. Roxanne had taught her how to make it seem like her eyes were connecting to his, whomever he may be for the night. Just wait for the sign. Accent the position with a poke of the hip. Look how smooth. Bend to the ankle of the pointed toe then roll up slowly. Was she calling to him? Tierra recalled Trigger's wink. Wherever she was, she saw his glare, his smirk. Was he calling to her?

Tierra trotted through the desolate street. Her gold colored sneakers squeaked in an offbeat rhythm, changing pace as she tried to steady her knees. They wanted to buckle beneath her, but shook out the tingles and kept on track. Droplets of sweat raced down the side of her face. There were footsteps behind her matching her speed. As they became louder, she picked up her pace back to a jog.

It seemed her grandmother was the logical person to call. Her heart sank when she heard the voicemail. Defeated, she hung up. The tears were heavy and full of salt. She called again. Voicemail. For fear of dying without leaving behind her love, she left a message. "Gran, it's me. He's going to kill me if he catches me. I'm so sorry for being mad at you. If I don't make it somewhere safe, know that I love you. I love Mommy too. I'm so sorry. My roommate, Michelle, she'll know who. I can't say it on the street. He's got people on so many corners. I'm going to try and find someone to help me. But I love you." Hanging up, she felt the pull of her jaw. Her gums throbbed.

Waiting to cross the street, she thought to dodge the honking cars, but looked back over her shoulder and saw no one. Maybe the footsteps were as imaginary as the voice that would call her name. She checked the phone. No missed call. *Should I text Michelle? No, she wouldn't answer. Why would she? I wouldn't forgive me.*

Tierra made it two blocks away from the dormitory she once stayed. It was then that she became conscientious of her lack of attire. She had run at least two miles before she found an alleyway she thought was safe enough to pull on the leggings. The too tight hooded sweatshirt that wouldn't zip past the middle of her breasts was still what she wore beneath her coat. Her hair was in disarray. Then there were the bruised, swelling lids and open scars on her face. Her lip was scabbing. The security officer wouldn't let her to the staircase without deciding an incident report was needed. If it weren't for the chaos of half the dorm in the halls the night she left, she may not have made it out without being detained and assessed for disciplinary action then. If she could just get inside somewhere, she'd be safe.

Destitute, she searched the street for an answer. The streetlights offered no comfort or place to hide. They seemed to be serving as coded flashes of lights, as signal to Trigger or his associates where to find her.

Tierra's strands were falling from her head. With each one she swiped from ehr vision, she'd realize the detachment. Deciding the dorm wasn't her safest option; she continued on. Half a mile later, she figured it was safe to slow down. Still no vibrating call, no worried texts.

At least I know Trigger isn't chasing me. There was no way he would've run to keep up. His pride wouldn't let him comb the streets searching for a runaway dancer, would it? He hadn't tried to call. She wondered how long it took him to notice she was gone. Maybe he wasn't searching at all and was wishing her good riddance.

The bright flashing sign of Lucy's was in sight. Should she yell? Should she scream? Would anyone come to help her? With no certainty she concluded getting inside was her best bet.

Again, Tierra quickened her steps. One gold hoop still hung from her ear. A peek at the pavement revealed a shadow. It wasn't hers. She looked back. No face. Even the outline of the body wasn't clear enough to know if it was a man or woman.

Desperate to make it on the grounds, Tierra ran faster than she had all night. The back entrance was easiest. She could smell the marijuana burning in the air. Relieved, she imagined the habitual smokers would have the door cracked as they blew their anxieties into the wind. Upon arrival, the door was locked. She knocked, but no one opened. She pounded. Still no opening. With tears in her eyes she looked around. Strangely, there was no line around the front. Although the faces were new to her, she ventured over to inquire of one of the two security guards manning the front entrance.

Just as Tierra made it around the bend, a flood of patrons burst out of the doors, each yelling as though they, too, were being chased. The horde was overwhelming. Tierra tried forcing her way through to the guards, but she was easily swept up. Her weak knees, oxygen running low. Somehow in the shuffle, she found herself in the parking lot. Vehicles were peeling out. She saw Caden's. She couldn't spot him in through the fleeing chaos. Trying to get a look at the guards out front, Tierra could only see the opened doors and darting customers. The guards struggled to apprehend some of the men.

Tierra spotted Noodle. She tried calling her name. It was then she realized how loud her heart was thumping. The breath it took to scream, she couldn't afford. Folks eager to get to their designated rides pushed past her, spun her around. Her head was wading. Starting engines amplified, revving throughout her ligaments. More people pushed, some pulled. She leaned against the door of an SUV.

Four shots rang out. Two men charged another fumbling man out into the street. Police sirens blared. Tierra knew she'd need to flee too. She made a go for it. Her forehead met the glass of the side view mirror. A re-opened gash was dripping with her blood. The chaos around her quieted. Her legs finally gave way. As she drifted off to sleep she cried, "Oh please, not again."

Someone was pulling on her coat. Shaking her. Then slapping her cheeks. Her body was determined to stay limp. No curiosity. No searching of the mind to match any of the voices calling her name. Yet, there were arms, firm, refusing to let go. Her head was lifted.

"Here, grab her legs."

I'm so tired. Maybe it's the angels. Gran says God gives rest. I wonder if this is what it feels like. These could be the hands of my father. "Daddy?

28 SITTING STILL

Cracked eyelids and swollen skin, Tierra had finally awoken. Her head heavy like a sinking brick, she peered to the right and noticed the parted blinds. Shades of rouge, faded yellows, and burning rust; the sun was settling on the horizon. She groaned, "I'm not dead, am I?"

Caden towered over from side. "You're awake, I see. If you slept any longer they'd have to report it as a coma." He stroked the strands of hair whisking above her forehead.

Sitting up was a chore, but Tierra rocked herself forward nonetheless. *Hope Knows No Bounds* was stenciled across the opposing wall. Beside it was a small whiteboard listing the name, Jennifer, as the attending nurse. "So I'm in the hospital. Great. I suppose I should thank you for getting me here."

"I wish I could take credit, but I had to stay back to give a statement. We were all scared for you, though." He kissed her cheek.

"We?"

"Gang's all here," replied a voice from the far corner.

Michelle rose from the armchair where she had spent most of the day. She stood beside Caden. Taking Tierra's hand into hers, she focused on Tierra's wondering eyes. "I'm so sorry," she sniveled.

Tears welling up, Tierra's hands shook. "How could you apologize to me? I hurt you, your face."

"That wasn't you."

Just then, the door swung open. Cherish, with Madeline closely behind her bustled through. Cherish's eyes glossed at the sight of her daughter sitting upright. "Oh my God, Tierra!"

Madeline rushed over and hugged her granddaughter. "My goodness baby, I was so terrified."

Cherish teased the friends. "We leave the room for one minute and the two of you can't follow instructions. I specifically said call when she wakes. You're all fit to be friends, you know. All hard heads." She shooed them away from Tierra's bedside.

"Oh Cherish, leave them children alone. If it wasn't for Michelle taking my call, we wouldn't have even known what hospital she was in."

Cherish re-propped the pillows behind Tierra's head and smoothed over the blanket.

"Nervous hands," Madeline mumbled. She winked at Tierra's friends. There weren't enough words to leap from her tongue to express her gratitude for Michelle's willingness to stay at Tierra's bedside until she and Cherish could arrive. The whole ride to the hospital she wrestled with the guilt of letting Tierra walk out of her house during Christmas break. *How could I be mad at her not wanting to swallow truths neither Cherish or I had been willing to digest for all these years? Gave her money, clothes, and food but then starved the girl of compassion.*

There was a gentle knock at the door. Madeline cleared her throat. "Tierra, I don't want to upset you, but Jackson's here and he's been waiting to see you."

Caden chimed, "Crazy he happened to be at the club last night. He brought you to the hospital."

"And don't forget how he whooped Trigger's ass… Oh excuse me. I didn't mean to curse in front…"

Cherish grinned. "We understand." She turned to Tierra. "I should've told you the truth and for that I apologize. He is your biological father, but that doesn't negate the relationship you had with Brandon. You'll always be his little princess. No one's going to force you to have a relationship with Jackson."

Streams of tears rolling down her face, Tierra pressed her lids together, replying, "But he saved me. How could I not invite him in?"

ABOUT THE AUTHOR

Raised in Brooklyn, New York, Phoenix Ash currently resides with her husband and daughter in Delaware. A Wilkes University, M.A graduate, Phoenix is the life examining host of the podcast, Life As P, author of LongNeck Bottles (2017) and Avenue Song (2018). In all that she writes, Phoenix explores the power and vulnerabilities inherent to the woman experiences.

Made in the USA
Las Vegas, NV
06 January 2021

15450270R00189